DANCING THROUGH LIFE
BOOK ELEVEN

Amazing

PATRICIA M. ROBERTSON

Amazing

Patricia M. Robertson

Sometimes death comes early and unexpected, like an early November snow, landing upon trees still laden with leaves, breaking branches, knocking out power lines. Grace shivered as she looked across the snow-covered expanse while stepping out of her car. A hint of sickly, sweet decay assaulted her. She smelled death.

"Doctor! Over here. Hurry up!" she heard a voice tinged with urgency coming from the barn.

Grace pushed an unruly lock of brown hair back behind her ear where it had broken free of the elastic tie she had pulled her hair into when awakened from sleep. Her night to be on call. Why is it horses always wait until night to give birth? She knew it was their schedule, not hers; still, it would be nice to be able to schedule them for a time that wasn't two o'clock in the morning. Even four or five would be an improvement.

She hadn't realized Mr. Blackburn owned any horses. This wasn't a working farm. Lamar Blackburn had long since sold his stock and let his fields lie fallow, as his daughter didn't want to have anything to do with the family farm. He had sold his cattle years ago if she remembered right. What was he doing with a broodmare?

Hopefully she wasn't too late. With horses, once their water broke, you only had fifteen to forty-five minutes to deliver the foal before it suffocated. Most deliveries required none or minimal assistance. Mother Nature knew what to do. It was best if humans kept out of the way. Perhaps that was why they chose the middle of the night? To avoid human interference. Those rare times when there were complications, you had to act quickly. By the time the owner calls you've probably lost precious minutes, then there was the time driving. She ran to the barn.

"Something's wrong. What took you so long?" Old man Blackburn's face was creased with concern as he met her at the door. "I can feel a hoof but there's been no movement for at least fifteen minutes. The horse, she keeps straining, but nothing is happening."

Grace chose to ignore the accusation in his voice. Nothing that hadn't happened before when someone was worried about an animal. Grace lubricated her arm and inserted it into the birth canal, feeling the rhythmic pulse of the internal muscles as the mare tried to expel the foal. Yes, there was the hoof. Something was holding up the foal from sliding through. The foal was presenting backwards, hind legs first. One of the hoofs was caught against the mare's pelvis. She needed to push the hoof back inside, correct the position and deliver the foal posteriorly.

"How long has she been like this?" Grace asked Blackburn. She didn't wait for an answer, springing into action using all she had learned over eight years of study. There was no time to question what to do. She hoped she wasn't too late and was risking the mare's life to deliver a dead foal. She waited till muscles relaxed then pushed the hoof into the uterus, twisted the limb so that the hind legs slid out together. The mare whinnied.

"It's all right, girl," Grace reassured the horse then slipped her hand back inside. Grace had the advantage of small hands that slid easily into the space, making up for her lack of strength. It was an advantage of being a female in a field once dominated by men. She helped ease the hips through then stood back as the rest of the foal followed. The foal was expelled and lay in a lifeless lump on the straw.

The entire barn was still as though the whole world was holding its breath, waiting. The mare lay where she was, spent. Not moving. And then she rolled, groaning with effort, slowly coming about until her long slender nose came into contact with the foal. She sniffed, then licked. The foal shook its head alert.

Grace breathed, unaware at first that she had been holding her breath. She had been wrong. Death would have to wait for another day. She was often wrong, but counted it as no loss when she was. She would rather be wrong than right when it came to premonitions of death.

"Your mare's okay. You have a beautiful colt." Grace had forgotten about the owner as she focused on the mare and foal. When he didn't respond, Grace looked over.

Blackburn wasn't there. She realized she hadn't heard him say a word since she started to work on the delivery. He wasn't standing in the stall where she had left him. He was laying on the hay, his hands clutching his chest.

Maybe she hadn't been wrong.

Chapter 2

Grace stopped in between the two exam rooms at the clinic to make notes on a chart. From the reception area she could hear voices.

"Is the doctor in?" a deep voice questioned.

"Which one, Dr. Bennet or Dr. Reese?" her receptionist countered.

"Dr. Reese, I believe."

"Do you have an appointment?"

"Look, I just need to talk to him, just for a minute." It was a strong, take-charge voice. The voice of someone who wouldn't take no for an answer. What did he want?

"It's her. Dr. Reese is a woman." Adah, her trusty receptionist wasn't going to be pushed about by anyone. Good for her. Grace could always count on her. She was the first line of defense in the office. No one got past her without being properly assessed. She had a way of putting people in their place. "Sit down and I'll see if Dr. Reese is available."

Dr. Reese, oh wait, that was her. Grace looked at the metal name tag pinned to her white lab coat. Yes, that was her. It was still hard to recognize that the person they had been talking about was actually her. Not possible. All those grueling years of study. Four years as an undergrad, four more in vet school. Despite all her work, she still felt like an imposter. Any day now, someone from the licensing bureau would come and take her license from her. Perhaps today. Maybe that's what this man was here for. She had better finish her paperwork while she still could.

"Someone here to see you," her receptionist interrupted her thoughts.

Grace finished jotting down notes from the patient she had just seen. Routine visit, check-up and heartworm test, twenty-pound, Beagle.

"Doctor," she heard her receptionist but didn't answer. "Grace." This time she responded. Grace didn't stand on ceremony with the staff. They had known her all along, first as the inexperienced volunteer, then the nervous vet student. They had known her as Grace long before she had become Dr. Reese.

Grace looked up from her chart. "Yes?"

"There's someone here to see you. Do you have time? He said it would just be a minute." Grace caught the frown on the dark face.

Grace looked at her watch. She was behind. Her next patient, a tabby cat, had been waiting for twenty minutes already. The look on her receptionist's face and the sound of the man's voice forced her decision. Tabby would have to wait a little while longer.

"Okay, bring him to my office." She sat down the Lab's chart and picked up Tabby's before walking into the office she shared with the vet who owned the practice, Dr. Jill Bennet, mother of her best friend Josie.

The man walked into the room and immediately filled the space with his presence. A stylish black overcoat framed his build. He had never been there before and yet he owned the space. "Dr. Reese, I'm Abel, Lamar Blackburn's grandson. I just came by to thank you."

"Oh." Grace accepted his outstretched hand, standing up and looking into deep brown eyes. A brown mustache graced his lips. Her hand felt small in his enveloping grasp. Her head barely reached past his chin. Why did she suddenly feel inadequate and small as he gazed at her? She pushed a stray lock of hair behind her ear. "I didn't do much. How is he doing?"

"Thanks to you, he's alive." Abel's gentle eyes were trustworthy despite his gruff, no-nonsense manor and appearance. She expected he was someone of importance from the way he commandeered the room, filling the space with his bulk and demeanor and owning the room, as if it were her, not him, who was the intruder. "He had triple by-pass surgery but is doing well. If you hadn't been there that night, he never would have made it."

"I'm glad he's well." Grace had checked on him that other night at the farm. She hadn't wanted to, was afraid of being right when she wanted to be wrong. She hadn't been able to detect any breathing when she had called 911, but what did she know? Her patients had fur, feathers and rawhide for skin. She didn't know how to diagnose a human with their flimsy thin skin. She had called the hospital later the next day. HIPAA rules. She wasn't able to get any information but at least he was on the patient registration. That meant he wasn't in the morgue. Not yet anyway.

"I also want to thank you for taking care of grandpa's horses and pay you for your trouble."

When Grace realized Mr. Blackburn was alone on the farm, she had made a point of stopping by twice a day on her way to and from work, to feed the horses and check on the mare and colt. Mother and son were doing well. She had been surprised to find another mare in the barn. She ran her hand over the smooth coat. Was it possible this mare was pregnant? She couldn't know for sure without testing. What was Mr. Blackburn planning on doing with three, possibly four, horses?

"That's all right, Mr. Blackburn."

"Barton. Abel Barton."

"We'll bill your grandfather for the labor and delivery. The feeding and follow up, I took upon myself to do. No charge."

"Nonsense. We'll pay you for your time. It's the least we can do. I'll take care of it on my way out."

"Will you be staying at the farm?" She felt a stab of curiosity, followed by a letdown when he answered.

"No, but my brother will be. He'll take care of tending to my grandfather's horses for now, until we decide what to do with them."

"Decide what to do?"

"Clearly my grandfather is in no shape to raise horses. For now, my brother will take care of them, until we can arrange for their sale."

Grace frowned at the thought of the horses being sold. She had already grown fond of them. But she told herself, that's how it goes. Mustn't get too attached. Mustn't let it affect her professional judgment. It was up to the owner to decide what happened to their animals. That was one of her hardest lessons while in vet school, harder than learning the anatomy of all those animals or pharmacology. What she could or couldn't do for an animal wasn't limited by her knowledge and science, but more often it was limited by the owner's checkbook and what they were willing and able to pay.

"If there's anything we can do for you …"

Having dispensed with his business, Grace could tell Mr. Barton was preparing to leave. He shifted his stance and glanced at his watch with the air of a man who had places to be and things to do. So did she. He put his hand in his inner coat pocket and pulled out a checkbook as he headed for the door.

"There is something."

Abel stopped and turned back to face her. "Yes, Dr. Reese?"

"She's a thoroughbred, both of the horses are. You know it's unusual for a mare to have a foal in November, even early November. Usually September is the latest. That tells me that she was bred early. I would like to check the other mare, see if she's pregnant and if so, how far along she is."

"Oh, I hadn't realized."

"She really should be examined and under a vet's care, just in case any problems arise. We didn't even know your grandfather had the one mare, much less two mares. The call had come as a complete surprise. Fortunately, no harm was done."

"My grandfather's old school. Must have figured he could handle them himself." His lip curled slightly upwards on one side as he shook his head. Clearly grandfather and grandson didn't always see eye-to-eye.

"Regardless, I would like to do a complete exam on the one mare, see if she is pregnant and follow up on the other mare and her colt."

Abel paused to think. He appeared to be running a calculator in his brain. Grace knew his type. Business man, doing a cost analysis, cost versus gain. Those brown eyes that had seemed gentle at first, now resembled a cash register — cha-ching, she could hear.

"If you're planning on selling them, they will need a clean bill of health from a vet." That seemed to settle it for him.

"Sure. My brother will be staying at the house. Call him and set it up. Tell him I said it was okay."

She stared at him as he cleared his throat and ran his hand through his thick hair. "Since you're footing the bill, I'd prefer to deal with you."

"No, I've got other business to attend to. Have to get back to my company in Chicago."

Chicago?

"My brother will be there. You can let him know your findings."

His tone was abrupt. What did she care? "Fine. Then I won't be seeing you." This time it was Grace who extended her hand. "Goodbye."

No loss, Grace thought as he walked out the door. At least she would still be able to see Coco and Peanut, the names she had given the mare and colt based on their coloring. And now she could do a complete inspection of Maple, the other mare. A small victory.

Grace truly cared for the health of her four-legged clients. It's why she had sacrificed to attend the best vet school she could, why she lived at home with her parents at an age when most women had already scraped up the money for a down payment on a home of their own. And who cared if Abel Barton wasn't there when she did her exam? He lived in Chicago, and therefore was what her college roommate would call GU, geographically undesirable. Moira, who was happily settled down with twins and a third baby on the way. The thought brought a pang. Sheesh, she told herself. It must be the breeding mare rubbing off on her. She snapped her notebook shut and nearly collided with her assistant.

"I'll see that tabby now," she said briskly.

"Already in room two," Adah replied.

Grace smiled. "Thanks."

"You need anything, boss?"

Grace was already on her way. "Like what?"

"I don't know, like a cool towel for your forehead?" The woman smiled and fanned her neck.

Grace frowned. "You don't mean?" She followed Adah's gaze to where Abel was putting his car in gear. A black BMW. As they watched, it roared off.

Adah giggled. "He's . . . "

Hot. "In a hurry," Grace said briskly. She gave Adah a look. She had won a small victory in getting permission to treat the horses at Blackburn farm, she reminded herself. Not that Abel was aware of any competition. If he had known she was sure he'd have not let her win so easily.

Chapter 3

Grace pulled up to the now familiar farmhouse. In the late afternoon light the place looked pleasant enough, though in need of attention. It had been two weeks since her encounter with the elder Blackburn grandson. Since then she had gotten to know the farm better, and Abel's brother. She honked her horn and headed to the barn. A young, slender man came out of the back door of the house, throwing a brown jacket on over his t-shirt and jeans.

It sure made it more pleasant to have Seth's company as she checked on the nursing mother and other mare. Seth always joined her in the barn, exchanging bits of information and pleasantries, making her laugh.

"How are my patients today?" Grace asked as Seth reached her, his long legs easily catching up to her. Seth Barton was different from his brother Abel. Where Abel was all business and serious, Seth was all fun, a jokester. Where Abel was dark and brooding, Seth was fair haired and carefree.

"Better now that you are here," Seth joked.

"Is that them or you?"

"Both. The world is a little brighter when you show up."

Grace knew it was flattery, but enjoyed it. After the intensity of pre-vet and then vet school, it felt good to relax, enjoy the fruits of her labor. "And you would know, after all your travels."

Seth had dropped out of school on several different occasions in order to "see the world," travelling by boat as a deckhand, cruising the Caribbean and the South China Sea, stopping at various ports of call, Melbourne, Singapore, Hong Kong, then on to Alaska and the Pacific coast. He often regaled her with his stories of danger and adventure while she checked on the horses.

"And who would have known all my travels would bring me back to Cascade Falls and to you."

Grace smiled despite herself, trying to ignore his comment as she got down to the business at hand. "Today I'm going to check Eleanor, see if she's pregnant." Grace patted the horse's rump. She had finally found out the horse's names. Fancy names befitting the thoroughbreds they were. Eleanor of Aquitaine, Lady Mercedes and Sir Perceval. It was hard to give up the names she had given them. What harm was there in holding on to those names? Soon they would be gone, sold to a farmer out of state. What did it matter if she called Eleanor, Maple, or Lady, Coco, or Perceval, Peanut? It was her game. One she played alone.

She was going to do the hand-up-the-butt check of Eleanor's uterus. After getting authorization to treat the mare – you just don't go around sticking your hand up a horse's butt without permission – she started her evaluation. Usually this procedure was used to check whether a horse was pregnant or not as well as to check for problems in internal organs.

She pulled on gloves, lubricated her arm and pushed it through the rectum to where she could feel the uterine wall. She noticed what felt like a foal, but there was something else there. Was it possible? Was she feeling two foals? Certainly, it was possible. Horses did have twins. But this wasn't good news, not at this late date. She estimated the foals were already close to five or six months. She would need to use an ultrasound to confirm this. Twins rarely survived, and if they survived the delivery, usually they were small and frail and didn't always make it past two weeks.

Grace pulled out her hand, removed the gloves, then vigorously washed off any remains of lubricant and horse stool, scrubbing each fingernail while she assessed the situation. One minute she had been happily chatting with Seth about nothing in particular, then the chatting stopped as she was deep in thought.

"What's up?" Seth asked. "Is something wrong?"

Grace continued to scrub her hands. "I think Eleanor is carrying twins," she finally said.

"Twins? That's great. Who doesn't like two for one?"

"Maybe when it's humans or a meal deal, but not for horses. The risk is too great."

"Then what do we do?"

"If she weren't so far along, we would abort the smaller of the two." Grace knew the procedure, though she had not done it herself. You reached in through the rectum, found the small mass of cells, then squeezed them till they popped, like popping a pimple, or a blister, only in this case it was a fetus. It had sounded so cavalier when she first read about it, but it was a procedure designed to save lives. The risk to the mother and both babies was too great. You risked losing all three if you didn't do anything. Often nature took care of it for you. The smaller one would die and be absorbed into the remaining twin. Or there was a spontaneous abortion. But once they reached this size, it was too dangerous to abort. You risked losing both foals.

"Well, if that's the treatment, I'm glad we can't do it," Seth said.

"It's not as simple as that. This is a high-risk pregnancy. We could lose Eleanor along with her babies."

"Not with a great vet like you," Seth assured her. She had no such assurance.

"And even if the foals deliver safely, they will be small and may not survive."

"We'll do what we have to do to keep them alive," Seth insisted.

"That we will," Grace agreed but she knew it would be more difficult than Seth realized. "What will your brother say? He's in charge while your grandfather recovers." Selling a mare pregnant with twins was not going to happen. How much money would he be willing to put into keeping them alive and healthy?

"What does it matter? Abel's in charge only if Grandpa isn't able to make decision. I'll talk to Gramps about it."

Grace left Seth to deal with his family, something she couldn't do. What she could do, though, was get Jill involved. She was more experienced with horses. Grace could use a second opinion.

Chapter 4

Grace poked at the pork chop on her plate.

"Is something wrong? Aren't you feeling okay?" Leave it to her stepmother Ava to know something was wrong. Her dad was usually oblivious, or if he wasn't, he chose not to say anything.

"Ava is so much better at these things," he used to say when she would try to talk to him. Ava was better, but sometimes a girl needed to talk to her dad. Fortunately, this wasn't one of those occasions.

"The mare at Blackburn farm, the one that's pregnant, she has twins."

"That's good news, isn't it?" Ava asked.

"Only if they survive. They are just as likely to die and take their mother with them."

"Then I guess that's not good news."

"Is there anything that can be done?" her dad asked.

"Not this late in the pregnancy. If old man Blackburn hadn't been so cheap and had brought her in sooner, we could have aborted one fetus, giving the other a fighting chance for survival, as well as the mother. It's a standard procedure in such cases."

"I know old man Blackburn, as you call him. He's a good man. Old school though. I've done work at his farm. Installed the plumbing out to the barn. It tore him up something terrible when he had to give up farming. He just couldn't make it on his own, with no kids around to help. His only daughter moved away when she graduated from high school. Was some kind of a scandal, or a fight, or something. Blackburn never talks about it."

"Moved away and never looked back, like Jacob and Ashley, only Ashley didn't even wait to graduate," Ava commented with a frown.

Ashley, her sister, had completed her senior year online and left to attend Juilliard in New York at seventeen. Jacob, her brother, was in California, playing basketball with the Golden State Warriors and dating her best friend, Josie.

"We're lucky to have you," her dad said. Grace knew what was coming next. "Our gift of Grace."

"Yeah, Dad. Lucky." She was lucky, wasn't she? She was doing what she loved. If that required that she live with her parents a while longer, that was okay. It wouldn't be forever, though sometimes it felt like it would. She wondered what Abel would think of her still living with her parents. Now why did she think that? He was in Chicago and she was here. Why even think of him?

"It's not that bad here, is it?" Ava asked.

"No. I do love what I'm doing. And I know living here made that possible."

"That's my girl." Her dad squeezed her shoulder as he cleared his plate from the table. "What do we have for dessert?"

No, it wasn't bad. She loved working at the vet clinic with Josie's mom. She had started there in junior high, shadowing Jill. She figured it was Jill's connections that had gotten her into Michigan State University's College of Veterinary Medicine, one of the best and most sought-after in the country. Jill, and maybe her dad's prayers that one of his kids would remain close to home.

Veterinarian programs were very competitive, harder to get in than med schools. She hadn't been the smartest student in her pre-vet classes at MSU, but what she lacked in brains, she made up for in hard work. The experience working with Jill helped too. Still, she was competing with top scholars around the country, around the world as MSU had a high population of international students. It had come as no surprise when she didn't get in with her first application. What had surprised her was that she had made the wait list. All it would take was for someone to drop out or decide not to come. What person in their right mind would change their mind once they got accepted? Apparently, there was someone not in their right mind.

She'd never forget that phone call.

"Could I speak with Grace Reese?"

"This is her."

"Grace, this is Dr. Wentworth at the MSU College of Veterinary Medicine. I met you at your interview."

"Yes." Grace could barely get the word out. Her heart had floated up her chest and lodged somewhere in her windpipe.

"We have an opening. Are you still interested?"

Still interested? Was he kidding? And to think she had almost decided to settle on that school in Colorado.

"Ms. Reese, are you still there? Did you hear me?"

"Yes, Dr. Wentworth. Yes."

"Yes, you heard me, or yes, you're still interested?"

"Both. Yes to both."

"Good. We'll put a confirmation packet with further instructions in the mail. Congratulations and welcome."

Grace took deep breaths until her heart settled back down in her chest, then left her hiding place in her bedroom and went downstairs to the living room where Ava was grading papers and her dad was watching baseball on TV. She stood in front of the TV.

"Grace, you make a better door than a window," her dad stated.

"I got in."

"Got in where?" her dad asked. Ava stopped grading papers.

"To vet school at MSU."

"Honey, that's great news." Her dad got up and hugged her, followed by Ava.

"This calls for a celebration," Ava said. "Ice cream?"

"This calls for the Parlour. Let me get my car keys." Her dad picked up his keys from the cubby by the door where he usually placed them when he got home. "I'm so proud of you, and glad you'll be close to home."

"Way to spoil it, Dad," Grace teased.

"What? You aren't happy to be close to home? You'll be able to come home for weekends, vacations, even for an occasional weeknight dinner. Hey, you can even commute."

Even that, the thought of staying in Cascade Falls, didn't dampen her enthusiasm. She was going to one of the best vet schools in the country.

So, here she was in Cascade Falls, living with her parents. She could get a place of her own, except, she had thousands of dollars in school loans to pay off. Commuting had become a necessity in order to save what money she could. Her dad helped, but even with his assistance she still faced years of debt before she could think of moving out. Her pay increase at the clinic helped, but was not enough.

One step at a time, she reminded herself. Now that she was a bona-fide veterinarian, her next step would be to be able to afford a place of her own.

Chapter 5

Another reason for staying in Cascade Falls was her dad's mother, Grandma Esther. Grace hated the thought of leaving her.

Grandpop, her great grandfather, had died over five years ago. Jacob had been playing basketball in Europe at the time and Ashley had been in the middle of a new production so neither of them had come home for the funeral. She had been left representing all three of them. Grandma Mary and Grandpa Tom, her mother's parents, had died a year later. That left only Grandma Esther and Peter, Grandma's second husband. She had heard that deaths come in threes. That was the case that year, three deaths, three grandparents in the space of one year.

She was no stranger to death. Death in the form of euthanasia was a regular part of a vet's life. She appreciated MSU's emphasis on ethics in its College of Veterinary Medicine. Still some animals had to die in order to provide a new crop of trained veterinarians. There were cadavers to slice through in order to learn the parts of animal bodies. There were live animals from shelters where they were destined to be humanely "put to sleep," sent to the school so aspiring vets could practice on live specimens. Necessary evils they claim, for the greater good.

Yes, she was no stranger to death, having made its acquaintance at the age of two when her mother died. She wished she remembered her mother. She had a vague recollection of a woman with a turban on her head who smiled sweetly at her, but that was all she could remember. Perhaps there had been a time when her mother had held her and cradled her in her arms the way mothers do. Her mother did hold her when Grace crawled up into bed with her before she died.

Grace remembered that, being held as her mother told her she loved her.

There were other memories, half-memories, made up out of the bits and pieces that she had been told about her mother—that her mother loved to dance, danced with Ballet Magnificat when she was in her twenties, then started her own dance studio, Joy's School of Dance where her Aunt Kathleen worked, carrying on the family tradition. Grace had grown up at the studio, going there after school each day. Her grandmother and aunt had both worked there then. She had attended classes and been looked after by the parents of students. You might say she had an abundance of mothers in her life. There was no shortage of mother figures, just not the one she most wanted. Her own real mother. Ava, her stepmother, filled the role nicely, up to a point. Her grandmother was a second mother to her too. How could she miss that which she had never had? But she did.

She was the one who didn't cause any trouble. Ashley had been the prima donna since childhood, insisting on having her own way. Jacob, the trickster. Maybe her parents needed a break when she came along, an easy child after headstrong Ashley and troublemaker Jacob. She didn't know. Sometimes it was like she didn't exist. Ashley had sucked all of the oxygen out of the air. When she left, Jacob took over. Such was their presence.

She opted for a quieter life. There were advantages to not being seen. She could get away with things Ashley couldn't. She liked being left alone, to her own devices. And if she was noticed for doing something she wasn't supposed to, well, Dad and Ava didn't believe it.

No, she was content with her lot in life, at peace with it. She went along with the flow, until she didn't. She followed Josie's lead during high school, getting involved with environmental issues, but when it came to her own career, she knew she wanted to do something different.

She had thought about working with people. It seemed people liked her, talked to her. She didn't have to say a word. She was good with people, or so she was told. She had an affinity for those who were hurting. When her grandmother had a stroke over fifteen years ago, she had enjoyed visiting her at the rehab facility, making friends with other patients. When she met Josie, she knew something was different about her, that she ran funny, but that didn't matter to her. She didn't mind waiting for Josie when she couldn't keep up. She naturally was attracted to people who were different or hurting, just as she had been attracted to hurt animals in Josie's mom's clinic. She fell in love with animals at the clinic when she started to volunteer there. Her decision was made.

Now that she was no longer in school, Grace saw her grandma several times a week. Sometimes her grandma stopped by the clinic to say "hi" and drop off a piece of pie or homemade cookies. Other times Grace stopped by her grandma's apartment on the way home from work or after dinner. Most Sundays Grandma and Peter came over to her house or to Aunt Kathleen's house for dinner. Sometimes it was a pain, all of the family obligations, but she figured she would miss it if she moved away. She definitely would miss Grandma Esther.

"You got a minute?" Grandma let herself into Grace's office where Grace was checking her schedule.

"Always time for you, Grandma." Grace stood up and hugged her.

"I made cinnamon rolls this morning, more than Peter and I can eat. Thought you'd enjoy them." Grandma placed the plate of rolls on Grace's desk. "Where have you been keeping yourself lately?"

"Helping out at the Blackburn farm, Grandma. You know that."

"I guess I did. This doesn't have anything to do with that nice young man who's living there now?"

"What do you know about it?"

"Just what the members of the Ladies Guild told me."

"No, it has nothing to do with him, everything to do with two sweet mares and a feisty colt."

"Just checking."

"Don't worry, Grandma. If anything happens in the 'male' department, you'll be the first to know."

"That's all I needed to hear."

"Thank you for the cinnamon rolls. You sure Peter doesn't want some of them?"

"What Peter wants and what Peter needs are two different things. One cinnamon roll is plenty for him."

"Did I hear my name?" A good-sized man, well-proportioned for his age, walked in and sat himself down in the chair by her desk. "Hmmm, are those the cinnamon rolls from breakfast?"

Peter's heart attack fifteen years ago was not apparent, thanks to her grandma's good care and cooking. Best thing to happen to him, that is after his marriage, Peter claimed. The heart attack had been a wakeup call. Since then he had been taking better care of himself, exercising, eating less red meat. Her grandmother's stroke a year before Peter's heart attack was also hardly visible. She had since regained most of her ability, though she did forget things now and then, now more than then. She was a modern grandma, working out, playing pickle ball and eating a diet of fish or grilled chicken breasts and salad most days, except for when she baked, but that was more for her family than herself.

"Didn't I tell you to wait in the car?"

"And I told you not to take too long. We're going to be late."

"Where are you going?" Grace asked.

"Yoga class at the library. Remember, dear," Grandma addressed Peter, "you are never late for yoga class. Whenever you arrive you are right on time."

"That may be what Heidi says, but I prefer a few minutes to stretch and relax before Heidi puts us through our paces."

"I thought yoga was supposed to be relaxing," Grace said.

"It is, when you are done and doing your twenty minutes of corpse pose," Peter explained. "But that's after an hour of contortions."

"Okay, dear, let's go."

Peter looked at the cinnamon rolls again. "Did you leave any at home?"

"Now look who's making us late." Grandma Esther grabbed Peter by the elbow and pulled him out. "Oh, Grace, don't forget, apples this Sunday."

"Right, apple time. I nearly forgot."

That's right. The traditional baking of apple pies for Thanksgiving and prepping the rest of the apples to be put in the freezer. Another reason she remained in Cascade Falls. She had helped pick the apples in October; now it was time to freeze them so Grandma could make apples pies for Christmas and special occasions. Blackburn farm could wait.

"Unless you have something else to do?" Grandma's eyes sparkled. "That young Blackburn brother is quite handsome, isn't he?"

Grace rolled her eyes and shook her head.

Grandma laughed. "Old man Blackburn wasn't always old, you know. Why, I remember …"

Grace couldn't take it. "Grandma, no! And I'm not interested in him anyway." It was Abel who intrigued her. Seth was … just a diversion.

Grandma watched her and smiled. "Well, you've got a lot going on. You can join me this Sunday. Unless you have more work to do at the Blackburn farm."

"Wouldn't miss it." Grace walked her grandparents out. Once back inside the clinic she briefed Jill about the pregnancy.

"How far along is she?" Jill asked.

"It's hard to tell but I'm guessing she's due in March or April."

"Not much we can do. She's too far along to attempt to abort one foal. We'll just have to keep an eye on her. It's possible she will miscarry one of the foals."

"We?"

"I can't let you have all the fun. I'd like to examine her. Have you talked to Mr. Blackburn yet? We need to know what he wants done."

"Not yet. He came home this week. I'm hoping to talk to him this weekend."

"Good." Jill looked at the plate on Grace's desk. "Your grandma's cinnamon rolls?"

"Yes, help yourself."

"Doctor?" The receptionist knocked on the open door.

"Yes," both women answered. Jill laughed as she took a bite of gooey deliciousness.

"Mrs. Shackelford is here. Seems Pooks has gotten into her yarn again."

Grace and Jill exchanged glances.

"Your turn," Jill stated.

"Okay, tell her I'll be right there. And let the vet tech know to prep for surgery."

Chapter 6

Most of Grace's days were filled with routine. Feline and canine wellness checks, spaying and neutering, cases of vomiting and diarrhea.

And then there were those walk-in emergencies. Mrs. Shackelford had one such emergency with her cat Pooks every other month or so. Pooks had a penchant for swallowing anything that resembled string — dental floss, crotchet cotton, yarn and, of course, string. This string would then make its way through her abdominal organs, stretching out through the intestines to the colon where, unfortunately, it ended caught up in various organs, unable to complete its natural course. The more it twisted, the greater the chance of damage as it could pull tight and sever part of an organ, allowing fluid to leak into other parts of the body. Such had been the case the last time Mrs. Shackelford brought Pooks in.

Her patients couldn't tell her where it hurt so she needed to be able to read their body language to assist her in making her diagnosis. Pooks wasn't much help. She sat on the examination table licking her paws. She was a beautiful Persian with long hair, which hair also caused visits to the clinic when hair balls expanded in her stomach beyond a size to fit through the cat's digestive system. In the past Grace and Jill had found long strands of yarn from Mrs. Shackelford's knitting bag.

Grace walked over to Pooks and started to examine her, feeling along her ribs and peering down her throat. Pooks was oblivious to the poking and prodding. Been there, done that before. It was routine.

"What seems to be the problem?" Grace asked.

"Pooks has been throwing up all night and the wad of yarn she was playing with yesterday is gone."

"Mrs. Shackelford, we've talked to you about leaving string in any form where Pooks can get it."

"I know, but she loves to run and chase after small balls of yarn and unroll it. I couldn't bear to take it away from her."

Grace peered down the cat's throat again. "Well, I can't see anything. We'll have to x-ray her and see if there is an obstruction anywhere."

"Oh, dear, you don't think Pooks will need surgery again?"

"If she's swallowed a long strand of yarn, chances are it will not pass on its own. It could be twisted in her intestines somewhere, so yes, she'll need surgery. But let's take the x-ray first before coming to any conclusions." Grace had already come to her own conclusion but needed x-rays to confirm it and help her determine how to proceed.

Sure enough, there were several questionable spots linked together by the offending string-like material. Pooks was prepped for surgery while Grace attended to her first few patients.

"Surgery?" Jill asked as they passed each other. "Do you think you'll need an assist?"

"I'll let you know." Fortunately, the yarn hadn't been able to work its way past the stomach yet. A blessing. Rarely were you able to make just one incision in these cases. Grace cut into the stomach, cut the yarn and was able to carefully remove it without making another incision. Jill popped in while she was closing.

"No problem?"

"We were lucky this time. It hadn't travelled too far or done any damage."

Jill looked at the suture. "Nice work," she said, then went back to her patients.

The emergency surgery on Pooks put Grace behind on seeing her patients so she skipped lunch, munching on a cinnamon roll in between seeing patients. She only allowed herself a mini-break to gaze out the window at the same scene she had seen most of her life and sigh. She was now a bona-fide vet. She had reached her goal. What next? What was missing?

"Do you need help? You okay?" Jill interrupted Grace's revery, her gaze piercing. She could never hide from Jill, but that didn't stop Grace from trying.

"Just taking a breather." Grace popped the last bite of roll into her mouth and proceeded to her next patient.

By the time she was done for the day, she was famished. One last stop before heading home. Blackburn farm. She had told Seth she would stop on her way home.

"Does everyone get this great service?" Seth asked as he joined her on her walk to the barn.

"No, just special cases. I love seeing Maple, Coco and Peanut, er, I mean Eleanor, Lady and Percival."

"I like your names better. And what about me?"

"Well, sometimes you just have to put up with people …" Grace teased.

"Hey!" Seth laughed and punched her arm lightly. "My grandfather wants to talk to you."

"I thought we were going to do that this weekend."

"He wants to talk to you now."

"Okay, let me check the horses first, then I'll join you." What was this about? Grace put the question aside as she saw her horses. Peanut was growing stronger every day. Lady and Eleanor looked every bit the thoroughbreds that they were. She had finally adopted their rightful names, but Percival would always be Peanut to her. Seth must have brushed them today. He was taking nicely to his new responsibilities.

Seth and his grandfather were waiting for her in a room that would have been the parlor back when the house was first built. Now it was just a living room facing west, catching the last rays of sun as it set. She was shown in by the woman Abel had hired to help around the house and take care of his grandfather.

"He knew I wasn't up to the job," Seth had told her. "I'm not much of a cook and I'm not any good at cleaning house or being a nurse."

"Will you be staying for dinner?" the woman asked.

Dinner? She looked at Seth. Did he want her to stay? Was that the purpose of inviting her to the house? And if so, why didn't he say anything? Awkward. She ignored her growling stomach. When Seth didn't come to her rescue, she took care of it herself. "No, thank you. I've got dinner waiting for me at home. Thank you though."

"Then I'll be leaving. The table is set and dinner is staying warm in the oven."

"Thanks, Audrey," Seth said as she left.

Apparently dinner had not been on Seth's mind. Mr. Blackburn looked her up and down without saying a word.

"Here, Grace, have a seat." Seth pointed to a chair. "Would you like some tea?"

"That sounds good."

Seth poured tea for all while his grandfather continued to stare at Grace.

"I hope you're feeling better," Grace said.

"Much better. Thanks to you, I might add. I'm afraid I haven't properly thanked you for your help that night."

"No need to. I'm glad I was able to help."

"Yes, and now I see you have ingratiated yourself into the household."

"Sir?" Grace shook her head. What was this about?

"You're all Seth talks about. You and how you're taking care of my horses. How much is this going to cost me?"

Another awkward moment. What had Seth been saying about her? "No, no charge." She bit her lip and looked down. The visits broke up the monotony of long nights at home. "Just the ordinary charges for exams and follow up care. I'm not charging for house calls. I like coming here." She met the old man's stare.

"I see that."

"Are you sure now is a good time?" Grace leaned over and asked Seth.

"Sure it is." Seth assured her then turned to his grandfather. "Gramps, stop being so ornery. Tell Grace about the horses, your plans."

"You may not know this, but I grew up in Kentucky, on a horse farm. The farm couldn't support all of us kids. My oldest brother got the farm, my next brother a piece of property next to the farm, my sister married well and my remaining brother bought his own home. That left me. I decided to come north, to Detroit. I heard a man could make a good living in a factory making cars. I planned to save my money and buy my own farm one day. That was what I did. I dreamed of passing this farm onto my children, but I only had the one daughter and she would have nothing to do with the farm. Then I thought, maybe my grandsons." He frowned at Seth before continuing.

"When it became apparent that wasn't going to happen, I sold off the milk cows and steer I had and retired from farming. I planned on traveling with my wife, Seth's grandmother, but that wasn't to be either. She died before her time. Unexpected but it does happen."

"I'm so sorry for you."

The old man grunted. "That was ten years ago. It's just been me rattling around in the big empty house on land lying fallow, land meant for farming. So last year, I got to thinking. I don't know how many years I have left. All I want before I die is to raise horses again, just like down in Kentucky. That's why I bought those two mares. Had them bred before they brought them up here from Kentucky. First Lady, then Eleanor. Thoroughbreds. As fine a pair as man could want. All I want is to be able to look out my window and see them grazing in the field. Is that too much to ask?"

"No, sir, not at all," Grace said.

"But I guess I didn't figure on there being complications. Back in Kentucky, we took care of our horses ourselves. And if there were problems, we had someone on the farm trained to take care of those problems. Only in the worst circumstances did we call for a vet." He gazed beyond her, out the window. Dusk was fast eating up the last rays of light.

"That's why I didn't call for you, not until I needed you. Now, my grandson is telling me the other mare has twin foals and it's dangerous."

"It can be, sir."

"What will it take to bring those foals to delivery and beyond?"

"I don't know sir, but I'm happy to help."

"I understand that the foals will be small and likely not worth much as race horses."

"That's correct."

Blackburn reflected on this response. "That's okay. It's not so much about the money. What can someone my age do with money but leave it to my grandkids?" He nodded in Seth's direction. "I just want to see horses living on my farm before I die, and if a grandson chose to live here and take it over, that would be good too."

"Gramps, I'm not fixing on you leaving any time soon," Seth said.

"Anyway," the man looked back at Grace. "What I'm saying is, I'm not looking to sell these horses any time soon and I'd like you to help with the delivery of the twins."

"That would be amazing."

"Amazing? Why do young people today always speak in hyperbole?" the old man snorted. "I'm delighted too, now get out of here so I can eat my dinner before it gets cold."

Seth walked Grace to her car. "See, I told you now was a good time."

"I wasn't sure at first, but yes, it was a good time. It worked out."

"And so, you're hired. It doesn't matter what Abel might say. How about we celebrate over dinner this weekend? My treat."

"Dinner would be nice," Grace responded. Was this a date? With the charming Seth Barton? Not his less than pleasant brother, Abel. Grace bit her lip and smiled, trying to appear appropriately pleased yet not overly excited.

Grace let out a deep breath and smiled once she got in her car. She had a date. Still she figured she wasn't done with Abel Barton yet.

Chapter 7

Grace met Seth at Hot Diggity Dog – the specialty hot dog restaurant downtown. She wasn't ready to deal with introducing Seth to her dad. This was more convenient. She could leave when she wanted.

The mixture of Thousand Island dressing and sauerkraut on her Reuben hot dog slipped over the edge of her bun onto her fingers. Reuben dogs were not ones to be eaten daintily. Seth reached over to wipe the mixture from the corner of her mouth as she reached up herself, their fingers lightly touching.

"Sorry. Messy dogs." Grace blushed at his touch.

"I'm not sorry. Here, let me get another spot." Seth leaned in to wipe the sauce away.

"Mr. Barton, I do believe you're flirting with me," Grace stated as she watched the enthusiasm with which he finished his meal. Seth downed two Coney dogs in the time it took her to finish her Reuben dog, then finished off the French fries and onion rings they were sharing.

"And if I am?" Seth licked sauce off his fingers.

"Nothing. Nothing wrong with it. I just wanted to confirm it."

"Confirm it with this." He leaned over and kissed her on the cheek. "Does that feel like flirting to you?"

Grace looked around the restaurant, everywhere but at him. She felt exposed under the bright lights and the crowd of teenagers and families with young children. Not exactly the most romantic spot in Cascade Falls, but it was like Seth — casual, nonchalant, fun. It wasn't that she had never been on a date before, just never with someone so bold. She wasn't sure what she thought of it.

"Come on." Seth paid the bill then took her by her hand. "The night is still young."

"Where are we going?" Grace hadn't realized the date included more than a meal; hadn't even been sure it was a date. Yes, they had exchanged pleasantries, all while she checked the horses, but nothing to indicate he was interested in being more than friends. Until now.

"I thought about the ax-throwing bar, but that didn't seem like you. Neither did bowling. So we are going next door."

"Next door?"

"No more questions. You'll ruin the surprise. Close your eyes." He took her hand. "Close your eyes," he repeated as she resisted. "Trust me. I won't lead you astray or let you fall."

"Okay," Grace agreed but the word slipped out between clenched teeth. This reminded her too much of her brother Jacob's tricks when they were kids. He would tell her to trust him, then she would feel water poured over her head or being shot in her face from a water pistol as he laughed at how gullible she was. All "big brother" stuff. She knew she could count on him in a pinch.

Grace tripped as her foot hit an uneven spot in the sidewalk. She felt Seth's arm wrap around her waist.

"You did that on purpose, didn't you?"

"And if I did, can you blame me?" He squeezed her briefly before letting her go.

"How much further?"

"We're here." Seth opened a door. "You can open your eyes now."

Grace opened her eyes to a darkened bar. Was this Seth's idea of a good time? A murky bar? Then she saw two pianos sitting up on stands at the back of the bar.

"Dueling pianos. You do like music, don't you? We never really talked about it, but you just struck me as the type to like music. I mean, who doesn't like music?"

Grace laughed. "Yes, I like music." What she didn't say was that the music she was most familiar with was church music and the classical music from the dance studio. What else she didn't say was that she had only been in a bar once before this. Bars had not been a part of her life growing up. Her dad and Ava never frequented them, as far as she knew. And they definitely didn't take her to one, even if the food was outstanding.

Her one and only experience with bars had been during college. That had been a bust as her roommate had left her at their table to sip her lonely Coke and fend off unwanted advances from men she didn't know and had no interest in knowing. After that, she stuck to parties at the dorm where she knew people and had an easy exit if she wanted one. Then throughout vet school she had been living at home to save money. Not a lot of opportunity for late nights out living under the watchful eyes of her dad and stepmom. Not that they would oppose her dating. They would have been happy for her. They just would have wanted to meet the young man and question him as to his intentions. Her sister Ashley had no idea what Grace put up with, what she had escaped when she moved to New York. Her dad would have checked on Seth, wanted to know whether he went to church, what he did for a living.

"Hey, I can't have just anyone go out with my precious little girl."

Only boys from church were acceptable, but those were limited and getting increasingly fewer as so many of the men her age had already married or were happily paired in a relationship. At least she had her animals and her career.

Seth led her to a table, then came back with two beers. "You do drink beer, don't you? I believe that came up in a conversation."

"No, not really." Now and then she shared a cold beer with her dad on a hot day, especially if she'd been out in barns and fields doing house calls, or after a long day at the clinic. But that was the extent of her drinking.

"Sorry. What can I get you?"

"Water's fine for now."

Seth sat down as the two piano players prepared to start. This was much more pleasant than the bar in East Lansing. It wasn't as crowded or loud. There was no pressure to dance. She could just sit and enjoy the music. She didn't remember when she had last had a night out. Not since the last time Josie had come home to visit.

Seth excused himself. Grace figured he was getting her a drink, until she saw him next to one of the piano players. Seth slipped onto the bench, taking the place of the other as he stood up and sauntered over to the bar. What was Seth doing?

"This is dedicated to the cutest veterinarian in town, sitting over at the table in the corner." He pointed in her direction and launched into a medley of love songs, with the other piano player easily picking up on the songs, playing along, alternating between songs, going faster with each one. They started with classic songs like, "The Way You Look Tonight" and "My Funny Valentine," then moved to more recent numbers. She had cringed when Seth pointed her out. She was not one to like the spotlight, preferred to hide in the shadows.

They finished the medley, then Seth started to play and sing the song, "You Light Up My Life." He finished to applause. The first piano player reclaimed his spot.

"Thank you to Seth Barton. Let's give him another round of applause."

Seth bowed and waved to the crowd in the bar.

"I didn't know you played piano and sang," Grace commented when he rejoined her.

"Just a few of the many things you don't know about me. I plan for that to change, just as I plan to get to know you better."

Grace hid behind her glass of water, raising it to her lips and taking a sip. "Maybe," she said, "but now, I have to get home."

"So soon?"

"Soon? It's almost eleven."

"Do you have a curfew?'

"No, of course not."

"Then what's the problem? Stay up with me. Let's watch the sun rise together."

"I have church tomorrow."

"Then just a while longer. What will it hurt?"

"Okay, just a while. Where to now?"

"A place I know. You'll love it. I'll drive."

Grace left her car downtown and rode with Seth. When he pulled into the drive to Blackburn farm she protested, "I thought you were taking me to a place you know."

"I am. It's a place you know too, but you've never seen it the way I have." He led her to the highest point of the farm where they could see an expanse of stars in the moonless sky. Off in the distance were lights from town.

"Beautiful, isn't it?" Seth stepped forward under the starlit sky, then spoke the words,

"Come near, that no more blinded by man's fate,
I find under the boughs of love and hate,
In all poor foolish things that live a day,
Eternal beauty wandering on her way."

Her eyes widened as she listened. "Yeats?"

He smiled, his eyes glinting in the moonlight. "I studied some poetry. I majored in philosophy during one of my stints in college."

Grace considered this as she looked across the expanse of the field below and the stars above, looking everywhere but at him. She didn't need to look at him. She was all too aware of his presence. The world was slowly rotating, shifting under her feet, and at its center, quiet and still, were the two of them.

"It's not every day you meet someone who quotes WB Yeats." She had meant it to lighten the air about them, but it came out ... serious.

"It's not every day you meet a woman who knows Yeats."

Grace shivered in the crisp autumn air. Seth reached his arm around her, pulling her close to warm her as they gazed together at the beauty before them.

"Did you know, in the medieval view, all beauty derived from the beauty of God?"

"I know now." Grace wanted the moment to go on forever, warm in his arm, inspired by the loveliness surrounding them. "So, this is what you wanted me to see?"

"Yes, you can go now." Seth lightly teased. Neither moved.

"What if this time I'm the one who doesn't want to leave?"

"But you have church."

"That's not till morning. Besides, this is church." Seth continued to warm her with his body. She didn't want to leave. Wanted to stay all night. "*To you I raise my eyes, to you enthroned in Heaven*. Psalms. That's the extent of my poetry."

"I must insist. I don't want to get on your dad's bad side by keeping his daughter out all night. But first, one more thing." Seth pulled her closer and caressed her face with his hands as their lips met. "I've been wanting to do that all night."

"Why didn't you?"

"I was waiting for the perfect time."

"And now?" Grace caught her breath, her lips burning in anticipation of another kiss.

"And now, I drive you back to your car so you can go home." Seth held her hand and steadied her as they walked back across the uneven ground.

Chapter 8

Grace rolled over in bed. Somewhere a voice penetrated the covers.

"Grace, are you coming to church?" Her dad. What time was it? She grabbed her phone. Ten already. She had set her alarm for nine. What happened? She must have rolled over, turned off the alarm and went back to sleep. Getting to sleep last night had been a challenge. The events of the evening kept playing over in her head. Pleasant reminders of an exceptional evening. Once she finally got to sleep, she hadn't wanted to wake up.

"Sorry, Dad. I'll meet you there," she shouted.

"Okay. Don't forget, we're going to your aunt Kathleen's after church for dinner and to help Grandma with her apples."

Apples, yeah, right. She had agreed to that, hadn't she? But that was then, this was now. The last thing she wanted to do today was peel apples for pie. She didn't want to go to church either. All she wanted to do was lie in bed and think about last night.

What a night. She didn't know how she had made it home. The drive was a blur. A drunken blur, but not from anything she drank. She was drunk on love, had never felt quite like this before. There had been school-girl crushes and boys who had been friends, but none of them had blossomed into romance. The few dates she had gone on had never amounted to much either. She wondered, was it her? Was she just too career-oriented as her dad had suggested? Did she send out these negative vibes to the men around her indicating she wasn't available? She knew it wasn't that she wasn't open to talking to new people. Strangers often opened up to her with no warning. She was approachable, maybe too approachable, her friend Josie had suggested.

"You're like a magnet for sob stories."

"What do you mean?"

"I mean, anybody with a sad story, they always end up talking to you, using up your time. By the end of the night you've spent the whole time listening to them instead of meeting other people."

Her dorm roommate Moira had been less diplomatic. "You're a loser magnet. You go to a party with one hundred new and interesting people to meet and somehow you always end up with the most pathetic loser in the room, no offense."

Could she help it if she was nice? Isn't that how you were supposed to be? What the Christian gospel demands?

"It's one thing to be nice. Another to be a doormat," Moira had continued.

She didn't know why. She liked being needed. She didn't like conflict, didn't argue with Moira, but wasn't surprised when Moira moved into another room with another roommate, one more suited to her party lifestyle. It seems Grace was holding her back. Grace's new roommate was even quieter than her, if that was possible. A fellow loser. At least there was no more pressure to go out and party. Grace was pretty much left to herself. Not what she had wanted but she was okay with it.

She had reassured herself that once she was through with her studies there would be time enough for dating, still there remained a part of her that wondered if she would ever find someone.

But last night. That was new. She wanted to relish the feeling like the last bite of hot fudge and caramel in a turtle pecan sundae or the foam on the top of her favorite latte. Should she call him? No, that was the hangover talking. If she called, she would break the spell and find out it wasn't all she thought it was. Perhaps he had only been playing with her, filling time while helping his grandfather. Soon he would be gone, off to his next adventure, and she would be left with a heart in need of repair.

She wanted to climb back in bed, instead took a quick shower and dressed for church, pulling her hair back into her signature pony tail. Why bother with trying anything new? Seth wouldn't be there.

Grace slipped past Pastor Joe and down the aisle, joining her dad and stepmother in their customary pew, the same pew she had been sitting in all of her twenty-six years of life. She had considered trying to find a new church, one with more people her age, or even going the route that Ashley and Jacob had taken and stop attending, but the effort just wasn't worth it. She had skipped church when she was in college, living on campus, but whenever she was home, she found herself back in this same pew. This was family, people she had known all her life. It was a second home to her, what with her family in attendance and her uncle Joe the pastor.

Grace cast a side-long glance at her cell phone throughout the service. No calls, no texts. Grace wanted to call Seth, but did she dare? What was the protocol for such situations? She didn't know. She was disappointed when there was no call or text on her phone after church, or after Sunday dinner at Aunt Kathleen's and helping Grandma peel apples. She decided to stop by Blackburn farm on her way home, just checking up on her charges.

"You know you're not fooling anyone." She could hear Josie as if she were in the car with her. "Everyone knows there's more reason for you stopping at Blackburn farm than just checking up on those horses."

"And if there is, so what? What does it matter to them?"

"I'm not saying I disapprove. I just want you to admit it. You like this Seth person."

"And if I do?"

"That's great. I only hope he recognizes how awesome you are."

She hoped so too. Dare she admit how much she liked him? One kiss and she had forgotten his brother, Abel.

She went over to the corral where the two mares and young colt were quietly grazing. The early November snow had not lasted. The horses were enjoying being out of the confines of their stalls. Grace climbed the fence in order to have a better look at them. They would need to be brought into the barn, fed, and bedded down for the night.

"Hey, you."

Grace didn't turn at the sound of his voice. She knew it was Seth, recognized his footsteps. She wished she hadn't eaten so much at dinner as her stomach churned. Seth climbed on the fence next to her.

"Hey, yourself." Grace continued to gaze at the horses.

"I've got great news."

"You do?"

"Yes. There's a horse clinic in Kentucky next weekend. We're going."

Grace glanced over at him. He was kidding … right? "Next weekend? That's Thanksgiving."

"Just for the weekend, Saturday and Sunday. We can leave early Saturday morning, stay overnight, then leave after the last session on Sunday, or before that if necessary. You aren't working, are you?"

"No." The clinic was closed for the holiday. "Who's going to take care of the horses while you're gone? Your grandfather still isn't strong enough."

"My brother's coming for the weekend. He can take care of them. It's the least he can do."

"But does he know anything about horses?"

"What's there to do? All he has to do is let them out in the morning and back in at night and feed them. It will only be two days. If Gramps wants me to help with these horses, I have to know more about them. I've been reading up on horses, on horse whispering. You want to learn more, don't you? It'll be fun."

"Sure." She did want to learn, but going away overnight? "Seth, about last night …"

"Don't worry about that. I'll be a perfect gentleman. There's a campground where the clinic is being held. We'll have separate tents."

That wasn't what she was wondering about. She sighed and bit her lip.

Chapter 9

Thanksgiving with her family. Why should this year be any different from the previous, or the one before that, or the one before that?

There was a time when the family Thanksgiving had been held at her home. Grace didn't remember, but she had been told. Her mother had loved Thanksgiving and insisted on having the meal there even when she was battling cancer. Her dad had kept the tradition the first year after her death, but after that relinquished the holiday to Grandma Esther, who embraced the day and all that went with it, cleaning the house, getting the extra table and chairs from the basement, planning the meal — who was bringing what and where everyone would sit. When Grandma gave her house to Aunt Kathleen and Uncle Joe, they had inherited the holiday along with alternating Sunday dinners. Her dad and Ava shared in the Sunday dinner rotation.

Grace had never known a Thanksgiving dinner anywhere else or any way else. Didn't everybody celebrate turkey day like them, with turkey, stuffing, mashed potatoes and gravy, lots of gravy? There was that one time when Aunt Kathleen ruined the gravy. Grace didn't know how it happened; she just knew the day lives on in infamy in the annals of the family as "the year there was no gravy." Then there was fruit salad, green bean casserole, corn casserole, rolls and butter. And for dessert, oh, the pies. Two apple pies, cherry pie, blueberry pie, chocolate pecan pie, and, of course, pumpkin pie. It was a banquet to outdo a Dickens' feast. Even if all you did was eat a bite of everything, you'd be ready to pop a button before you took your first mouthful of pie. And that didn't take into account the appetizers — an assortment of cheeses and crackers, summer sausage and salami, shrimp, and fruit and veggies for dipping.

Peter always let out his belt a notch after dinner. "I'm in training for the holiday season," he would state as he rubbed his belly. "Someone has to be Santa. It's a tough job, but someone has to do it."

Her grandmother would frown and look over her glasses at him. Grandma knew he was joking. Since his heart attack Peter had lost thirty pounds or more and wasn't about to put it back on. Thanksgiving and Christmas were the only times he indulged and ate whatever he wanted, under Grandma's watchful eye. It was part of the tradition, a drama played out each year.

Some members of the family had moved on from the tradition. Ashley had come back a few times while in school, but once she started dancing professionally, she always had an excuse to keep her away over the holidays. After a while, her dad stopped asking. The same for Jacob. Once he graduated from college and went off in pursuit of his dream to play professional basketball he was rarely home for holidays. But some faces didn't change, they just got older. Her grandma and Peter, her dad and Ava, Aunt Kathleen and Uncle Joe. Her cousin Stephanie would be there, along with her son Gus, now a teenager, and maybe Stephanie's latest boyfriend. Her cousin Michelle was married and took turns coming to their Thanksgiving and going to her in-laws. Scott, one of Aunt Kathleen's sons, had married Alexandra, Alex for short, the daughter of Julia, Aunt Kathleen's best friend. Sometimes they all came, Scott and Alex and their kids, Julia and her husband Henry and their teenaged daughter Caroline. It gave Gus someone to hang out with. She heard her cousin Josh might show up. You never knew with him.

She wondered how Seth's Thanksgiving was going with his brother and grandfather. She had thought about inviting him to Thanksgiving. Dad and Ava were pushing to get to meet him, but not at Thanksgiving. Way too much pressure. She couldn't imagine introducing a boyfriend to her large, extended clan. Certainly, it would send him running, although Seth had expressed some interest in meeting her family.

"It must be nice to be part of a large family," he had said.

"You have family, don't you?"

"No, it's primarily my brother and me and Gramps."

"What about your parents?"

"My mother's off travelling the world with husband number three. She was never one for family holidays. Always wanted to spend the holiday in some place exciting and new. I can't imagine having the same tradition every year."

"What about your dad?"

"Husband number one? Gone. He left my mom shortly after I was born. Couldn't be tied down, I guess. He was a rover, like my mom. Abel was the closest to a father I had. At least my father married my mom, unlike Abel's father."

"I'm sorry. It must have been hard for you. You and Abel had different fathers?"

"Long story. Suffice it to say, my mother got knocked up in high school. When she refused to have an abortion and instead ran away with the man, my grandfather disowned her. Grandma managed to keep in touch with my mom, behind Gramps's back. She never had the strength to stand up to him. Still, she did send mom money now and then.

"When I came along, Grandma finally persuaded Gramps to recognize mom again and his grandsons, but it was short-lived. Gramps and my mom, they were always at odds. Grandma said it was because they were so much alike. When Grandma died, that was pretty much the end of my mother's relationship with my grandfather. At least by then, we had gotten to know Gramps. At one point we lived with Grandma and Gramps. That was back when our mother took up with husband number two. He didn't like kids so we were sent away. I didn't mind. I liked it here."

"What about your brother? Did he like it here?"

"Abel? I don't know about Abel. He never shared anything with me. He was in high school then, but he was still trying to be my father. He's like that. Always in charge, trying to run everyone's life."

Grace could see that, had felt that in the short exchange she had with him. Now she understood why. "I'm surprised I don't remember you from then. Cascade Falls isn't exactly a large city."

Seth shrugged. "Different schools. Different friends. Anyway, enough about my family. Your family sounds amazingly normal next to mine. I'd love to share a meal with a picket fence family like yours."

"Picket fence?"

"You know. The all-American family. White picket fence, two kids and a Suburban."

Grace had caught the hint but she wasn't about to invite him to Thanksgiving. Maybe a family Sunday dinner, Grace thought as she finished off her turkey, wiping the remaining gravy with a roll.

"Grace, you coming over this weekend so we can go Christmas shopping?" her grandma asked. Christmas shopping, not on Black Friday when it was crowded and crazy, but on the Saturday after Thanksgiving had become another tradition for her and her grandmother. How could she have forgotten it?

"Sorry, Grandma. I'm going to be gone this weekend."

"Gone?" Her dad's head arose at the word. "Where are you going?"

Grace squirmed as the room became quiet. The twenty-minute lull. Every twenty minutes there is a lull in conversation before it begins again. Why did the lull have to hit just then? Why didn't everybody continue their conversation? She hadn't mentioned being gone to her dad yet. This was not where she wanted to bring it up.

"No big deal. I'm going to a horse clinic in Kentucky."

"A horse clinic?" Ava asked.

"Yes, to learn techniques for handling horses."

"You mean like horse whispering?" Gus asked.

"Well, yes, horse whispering."

"Radical," Gus stated. "Can I come along?"

"Since when have you been interested in horse whispering? And what about the homework you are supposed to do over the weekend?" Stephanie asked.

"Since Grace is going to a clinic ..."

"This doesn't have anything to do with that homework assignment, does it? Don't you have a twenty-page research paper due next week?"

"Ah, Mom …"

"No way you're going away until your homework is done. You finish the paper — then you can talk to me about it. That is, if it's okay with Grace."

"I don't know," Grace said. "I have to see if there are tickets available."

"I wouldn't worry about it," Uncle Joe spoke up. "The chance that Gus here will have his homework done is minimal to non-existent."

"Come on, Grandpa."

"Just speaking the truth."

"What about me?" Caroline spoke up. "I have my homework done."

"How are you getting there?" Ava asked.

"I'm driving down with Seth," Grace said. "We're using his grandfather's car. We'll be staying at the campsite at the clinic."

"Oooh, Seth," Stephanie teased.

"I've been to those before," Julia said.

"Really? When?" Grace asked.

"Growing up in the south, every refined young lady knew how to ride a horse. Daddy kept a couple of horses at a stable not too far from our home. I used to ride my bike over after school."

"I should have known," Aunt Kathleen said. "Of course, you had a horse while growing up."

"Not much time to ride now, though I would like to someday. If the work load at the hospital ever lightens up."

"Maybe you could ride Eleanor or Lady sometime. It would be good exercise for them," Grace suggested.

"You and Seth don't ride them?"

"No, I've never ridden a horse yet, and Seth, I don't know why he doesn't. Guess he doesn't know either." The most she saw Seth do was brush their coats, feed them and lead them to and from the stable, now that she thought of it. She didn't have to ride a horse to treat it. But if Seth had lived with his grandfather for a while, why hadn't he learned to ride horses?

"What about me? Can I ride them?" Caroline asked.

"We'll see," Julia told her. "Maybe I'll come by and check them out sometime," she told Grace.

"Why go to a horse clinic if you don't ride horses?" Gus asked.

Good question. Why was she going? "I might be helping Seth train the colt, once he's big enough. Just because I don't ride horses now, doesn't mean I won't in the future. It also will be helpful for any veterinary work I might have with horses. Always good to know how to communicate with a horse, keep them quiet when you're examining them."

"Sounds like plenty good reasons to me," Peter said. "Not that she had to have any. Grace can make her own decisions. You don't have to justify them to us. Now how about we clear the table so we can have pie?"

Grace could always count on Peter to stand up for her. She was grateful he ended the conversation. Grandma stood up for her too, in a different way. At least now it was out in the open. She was going to Kentucky with Seth. No further need for discussion. Her dad looked over at her like he was going to say something, then thought better of it. Another reason to be grateful.

After dishes were washed, Grace went out onto the front porch to watch the younger kids play. Gus and Caroline were playing touch football with Scott's boys. The porch was a new addition to the house since Aunt Kathleen and Uncle Joe moved in. Grandma had always wanted one but never had the money between raising her own kids and then Aunt Kathleen's boys. Aunt Kathleen used the money she and Joe had been saving to buy a home to pay for the porch. Now it was a favorite gathering spot when the weather permitted.

"So, you and Seth?" Stephanie joined her on the porch, followed by Josh. "Are you an item?"

"By an item, if you mean, are we dating? We did go out once, so I guess that would be yes. What about you? Where's your latest? I thought Mike was coming?"

"We broke up."

"Oh, sorry for bringing it up."

"Don't be. It's just as well. He wasn't right for me."

"And who would be right for you, Miss Stephanie?" Josh teased. "Seems you've already gone through every single man your age in the county."

"And you've burned through all of the single women in Kalamazoo," Stephanie retorted.

"Oh, I think there's a few I haven't charmed yet. Though you do have a point. Maybe I need to broaden my horizons, start checking out the women in Cascade Falls."

"Good luck. Maybe I need to check out the single men in Kalamazoo."

"Couldn't hurt. I'm sure I could find a few for you."

"What happened to that young woman, what was her name?" Grandma spoke up from where she had been sitting in a rocking chair. "Shantilly or some such name?"

"Tiffany, and that was two girlfriends ago. Face it, Grandma. None of them compare to you. You have spoiled me for life as far as women are concerned. If I could find someone half as sweet and smart as you, I'd settle down."

"You're right there." Peter came out on the porch carrying Grandma's coat. "No one can hold a candle to this young filly. She's a thoroughbred."

"Don't be silly, Peter." Grandma willingly accepted the coat. "What's all this horse talk?"

"I was inspired by the conversation at dinner." He smiled at Grace. "Now it's time for these old horses to be put out to pasture."

"And time for me to head home too," Grace said, but first, she had to stop at Blackburn farm.

Chapter 10

Grace stretched her legs and rolled her shoulders after the long drive from Michigan to the Kentucky border. Seth found one of the few remaining parking spots in the lot closest to the arena. At least they didn't have to bring one of their horses. Hauling a trailer would have added time to their trip. Grace had fretted about this as she looked over information on the clinic.

"Don't we have to have a horse to work with?"

"No, that's for people who have a horse they want to work with. We could rent a horse if we want, or we can just watch and learn before trying the techniques."

"Okay, watch and learn. That I can handle. How do you know so much about this?"

"You forget. While you are gainfully employed at the clinic, I have all day to go online and read up on this stuff."

"I wondered what you did with all of your free time."

"Now you know."

Grace and Seth made their way to the arena where classes had already started.

"If we like what we see, we can schedule a clinic in the spring in Cascade Falls," Seth suggested.

"We don't have an arena."

"Relax, we can partner with another horse farm that has one. Then we can work with both mares."

They found a spot on the stands to sit and watch. The trainer was in the middle of a round pen. A horse circled around the edge. With a single click of his tongue and a wave of his hand, the horse picked up speed, then the trainer slowed her down. The horse approached him but he sent her back to run the edges of the corral. He talked the whole time, explaining everything he was doing, every hand gesture.

At one point he stopped and simply addressed those in attendance. "I trained with Buck Brannaman for years before going out on my own," he explained. "Buck used to say he didn't work with people who had horse problems, he works with horses that have people problems. Most problems in horses are related to people who don't understand their nature and go against that nature. Horses are beautiful, sensitive creatures. They are prey though, food for other animals in the wild. And so, they are always wondering, are you a predator? That's why they are skittish. You need to gain their trust and respect."

He brought the horse to the middle of the corral. This time he touched her nose, then rubbed her as he gained trust. "This is the first time this horse and I have met," he commented as he touched her.

"Horses are bilateral. See how their eyes are situated on either side of their head. They can only see on one side. If you stand on the right side, they only see you with that eye. They have no recollection of you on the other side. You have to let them see you on both sides."

Grace sat forward in her seat. She didn't want to miss anything as the trainer explained how even though he had never met this horse before, in twenty minutes he was handling the horse as if he had been working with her all her life. The horse was a two-year-old, never been ridden. Eventually he was going to train the horse for a rider.

Around her Grace could hear people saying, "Amazing," as he walked the horse through her paces. She didn't know enough about horses to realize just how amazing what he was doing was, but she was impressed. She looked at the brochure for the clinic. Brody McAdams was his name. He was listed as a horse whisperer.

They broke for lunch. That afternoon Brody was going to be working directly with attendees and their horses while others watched. Later he brought back the filly from the morning. This time he placed a blanket on her back.

"Remember, this is the first time she has had anything on her back." When she was comfortable with the blanket, he placed a saddle. Again Brody waited till the horse was comfortable with the weight on her back. He had the person who would eventually ride the horse introduce himself to her and rub her nose. Then he placed a mannequin on her back. When the horse was used to the weight of the mannequin, he introduced the rider to the horse in three steps. First the rider leaned on her back and came back down. Then he put a foot in the stirrup and leaned again before coming back down. Finally the rider was on her back, both feet in stirrups and ready to ride. All done with no bucking, no whinny of complaint. Those in attendance applauded.

When Brody worked with non-compliant horses, he would let them run around the pen, use up some energy, then use the same techniques he had displayed earlier to gain the horse's trust and respect. He would step forward and the horse would back up. Then he would back up and the horse would follow. The horse followed his lead like a dance partner. He even compared it to a dance.

Grace felt the hairs on her neck tingle as if responding to a long-forgotten call. She felt her mother's presence. Even though she had not known her mother, she knew that was what she was feeling. What else could it be? She had never been good at dancing but something told her she could learn to dance with horses.

Seth was not as enthralled as she was. He sat against the bleacher, leaning back on his elbows while she sat forward.

"Impressed?" he asked when the class ended and Grace sat back.

"Impressed." The word came out in a whisper.

"Glad I talked you into coming?"

"Definitely."

"Good. Do you think you could do what he did?"

"What he did? I'd never be that good, but I think I could do it."

"That's all I needed to hear. Let's sign him up for a clinic in Michigan."

"What?"

"You heard me. Let's see if he's available this spring." Before Grace could say anything else, Seth had jumped off the bleachers and was waiting among the crowd that had gathered around McAdams.

Grace joined Seth as the trainer spoke to each person with the same ease and grace that he had approached the horses. They waited for their turn.

Seth shook his hand and introduced himself and Grace. "We'd like to have you come to Michigan in the spring."

"You'll have to check with my scheduler. I may already have a clinic scheduled in Michigan." McAdams looked at Grace and shook her hand. "Do you train horses?"

"No, I don't even ride them. I'm a veterinarian. Your teaching will help me with the horses I treat."

"Shame. You should ride horses and train them. You're a natural. Come into the arena with me tomorrow. I'll introduce you to the horses."

Grace's mouth dropped open as she searched for words.

"Horse people always recognize other horse people." He tipped his hat then turned to the next person waiting to talk to him.

"She'll be there. Thank you," Seth told him.

"Did you hear that?" Seth said as they walked away. "You're a natural. I knew it. This is a great opportunity."

"But I have so little experience. There are so many people here with more experience with horses than me."

"But he picked you. You'll be great," he assured her as they made their way to the campsite for the evening.

If only she were so confident.

Chapter 11

Grace tried to recapture the feeling from that afternoon as she sat next to the campfire and listened to the horse people around her talk. Had it really been her mother? If not, then what?

The other attendees shared stories about other clinics they had attended. "He's good, almost as good as Buck Brannaman."

"Who's Buck Brannaman?" Grace asked.

"Didn't you see the movie, 'Horse Whisperer'? The techniques Robert Redford used in the movie, they're all Buck's. He helped with the movie."

Grace hadn't seen the movie, but determined she would.

"I think all this talk of 'whispering' is overrated," another woman sitting by the fire stated. "I think it should be called 'listening'. You have to learn to listen to your horse, understand what their movements are telling you."

"Gloria, that's part of horse whispering," the first woman stated. "It's not about telling the horse what to do but hearing the horse at a deep level."

"Well, I think they should be clearer about that. There are other horse trainers out there. Did you see the video about the man in France? Jean something. He rides bareback, stands on his horses. He's amazing." The chatter continued. Grace realized how little she knew about this aspect of working with horses. But where would she find the time to learn more? Being a vet was a demanding position.

She was so preoccupied with thoughts about all she had learned that day that she almost didn't notice when Seth settled into the car for the night, leaving her the tent she had brought. Almost, but not entirely.

She woke up stiff from all of the sitting yesterday and a night on the ground, but excited about another day of lessons. She hoped Brody forgot about having her work with the horses. It was just something you say, right? Telling someone to come into the arena. He couldn't have been serious. Grace settled back onto her spot on the bleachers, her ears primed to hear. She relaxed as McAdams continued with the lessons, giving no indication that he was looking for her to show up. Then at one point he stopped.

"There's a young woman here, a veterinarian. Where are you?"

Seth prodded her to get up. "She's right here," he shouted, pushing Grace forward.

"Come on into the arena with me," Brody told her.

Grace had no option but to go. Everyone had already seen her. She edged her way down the bleacher and into the arena and stood next to McAdams.

"Come here, what's your name again?"

"Grace. Grace Reese." Her voice sounded unnatural to her as she spoke, barely able to get the words out.

"And you're a veterinarian, right?"

"That's right."

"And you've never ridden a horse?"

"That's also right."

"Grace, what I'm going to do is show you and everybody here just how easy it is to learn how to work with horses using my methods. Does that sound okay to you?"

Grace gulped. "I guess so."

"No one is going to force you to do anything you don't want to do, any more than I force the horses I work with. Understand?"

"Yes." Grace started to feel at ease, as at ease as she could be out in the limelight, in front of all those people.

"Just listen to me and focus on the horse."

"Okay." She could do that. Grace focused on the horse in the arena with them as she listened to his instructions. Before she knew it, she was rubbing the horse on her nose and rubbing her down the way she did when she examined horses. This wasn't so bad. Then Brody showed her how to get the horse to follow her lead. The horse came forward, and then moved back as she approached. There she was, dancing with the horse. After putting the mare through her paces, Grace allowed the horse to approach her and rubbed her again.

"So, Grace, are you ready to ride?" McAdams asked her.

Grace rubbed the horse. It felt like the mare was inviting her to climb on her back, but suddenly Grace was all too aware of the people watching. She backed away. Not today.

"I don't think so."

People in the stand shouted encouragement to her. That made her more aware of their presence and more skittish.

"That's okay, Grace. Remember what I told you before we started. We don't force our horses to do anything they aren't ready to do, and we don't force our people either. You did great." He lightly touched her shoulder with his large hand. "Give a hand for Grace," he shouted to those watching. Grace walked back to the bleachers, the sound of applause in her ears.

Chapter 12

Back at the clinic after the long weekend, Grace kept glancing at the clock. One more appointment and she would be done for the day. So far, the day had been routine, two spays, one neutering, a wellness check and a cat with diarrhea. Pretty routine. Good. She was exhausted from the weekend.

They had left the horse clinic early, hoping to beat some of the holiday traffic. No luck. The drive back took two hours longer than the drive there, all in heavy traffic. It could have been worse. She could have been the one driving. As it was, Seth took it all with the good nature that was his trademark. No swearing at cars cutting him off, no tailgating. You can learn a lot about a person by how they drive in heavy traffic. Fortunately, the traffic eased up some once they hit the Michigan border and got off the interstate for less travelled roads. Unfortunately, it was already dark. No opportunity to enjoy the scenery. Just a sea of black, broken up by lights from houses, including random Christmas lights. Again, it could have been worse. They could have been hauling a horse trailer, or it could have been snowing or sleeting.

It had been a packed two days. Not quite what she had expected, though what she expected, she wasn't sure either. She had expected more time with Seth. Sure, they had all of those hours in the car but that wasn't the kind of time she had been looking for. There had been some repartee, another one of Seth's trademarks, she suspected. But no kisses, just a brief hand on her back as they moved from one spot to another. You couldn't kiss while driving and once they arrived at the horse clinic there were people everywhere, all around them. At the classes, over meals at the café that had been set up for the event, and at the campsite. She enjoyed the people and their stories. She just wished there had been a little time for just the two of them. She didn't even get a goodnight kiss before he climbed into the car, leaving her alone in her tent. He did surprise her, though, with a wake-up coffee and a quick hug in the morning. She guessed she had to settle for that.

She had thought she'd at least get a goodnight kiss once they were back at the farm. They pulled in after eleven. Not terribly late. The back-porch light was on. As they pulled up the gravel driveway, a figure loomed on the porch.

"Abel," Seth commented. "He's probably steaming. He has to be back in Chicago for work tomorrow."

"Couldn't he have left after the chores were done?"

"And risk that I might not make it home for morning chores? You don't know my brother."

Grace looked at the large menacing figure outlined against the porch light. She didn't think she wanted to know him.

Gone was the opportunity for a good night kiss. Seth climbed out of the car and waved to his brother. The dark figure grunted and went back into the house.

"Guess I better go in and face my brother."

"You didn't do anything wrong," Grace said from across the car.

"Tell him that. I think he's been angry ever since I was born. Maybe he was born that way," Seth muttered. The shadow from the porch appeared in a window. "Anyway, that's no concern of yours. See you tomorrow?"

"Sure." Grace got in her car and headed down the driveway back to home where a light had been left on for her, but no looming shadows. Everyone was safely asleep, or so she thought until surprised by her stepmother in her bathrobe coming out of the kitchen.

"Did you have a good time?"

"What are you doing up?"

"Couldn't sleep. Thought I'd get some warm milk, with a little cocoa, to help me sleep. How about you? Would you like some?"

Grace was tired, but she was also wound up. Cocoa sounded good. Was Ava looking for a one-on-one conversation? Grace wasn't sure she was up for that.

"Sounds good but I better get some sleep. I've got to get up for work tomorrow."

"Me too." Ava shrugged then started up the stairs. Was there a slouch to her shoulders, like she was sad about something? Maybe she should call her back, tell Ava she had changed her mind about the cocoa. Too late. She was already gone.

When Grace got up the next morning, Ava was the same as always.

"How was the clinic?" her dad asked.

"Good. Really good." Grace grabbed a coffee and headed for the door. "I've got to get to work."

"You can tell us about it tonight over dinner," Ava said.

"I may not be home in time for dinner. Don't wait for me."

"Then whenever you get home."

"Sure," Grace agreed. She always agreed, whether she wanted to or not. That was her trademark.

Despite not having the time with Seth that she had expected, she wasn't disappointed. It had been an amazing two days. She couldn't wait to try what she had learned on Lady and Eleanor. She had signed up for an online video course on the techniques McAdams had demonstrated and bought his book. She was trading in her text books for another learning opportunity. She knew it wasn't the same as having an instructor show her what she was doing, but it was something. She was about to leave the vet clinic when the receptionist stopped her.

"I'm sorry, Grace, but we have one more patient, an emergency."

"What is it?"

"The Peterson's cat. Seems she's been vomiting all day. Hasn't eaten anything either."

"Okay, bring them in." Vomiting could be caused by any number of reasons. It wasn't what she would necessarily call an emergency, but for the Petersons she was sure it was. They were an elderly couple, late eighties or early nineties she figured. That cat was the center of their lives. They had shared various pets throughout the years, all of whom were their babies. They had been old when Grace had first met them at the clinic fifteen years ago. Now they were ancient. She wondered how they kept going.

She was surprised when only Mrs. Peterson entered the room with Priscilla, their cat. They usually came together. It was their primary form of entertainment, one of the few excursions out of their home, this and doctor appointments.

"Mrs. Peterson, good to see you. Where's Mr. Peterson?"

"He's not feeling well."

"I'm sorry to hear that. Tell him I hope he's feeling better soon."

"I will."

Grace examined the tabby cat. "When did she start vomiting?"

"Just this morning."

"Did she get into anything? Eat anything she wasn't supposed to?"

"I don't know. She was outside. I think I saw her licking some stuff in the driveway, something greenish."

Grace didn't like the sound of that. She had talked to the Petersons before about what this cat could get into if they let her roam about outside.

"But she cries so if we keep her inside," Mrs. Peterson always said. "She doesn't go far, stays in our yard. I usually go out with her."

Once an indoor cat gets a taste for being outdoors it's hard to keep them inside. Could Priscilla have gotten into antifreeze? It's green and sweet. Sometimes if it leaks from a car radiator a cat will lick it. If so, Priscilla's chances weren't good.

"She appears to be dehydrated from vomiting. I can give her something but depending on what's causing the vomiting, it may be too late."

"What do we do then?"

"I'll see what I can do." Grace gave the cat an infusion. Priscilla was only six years old. She could easily live another ten years. But then, maybe she was wrong. Maybe Priscilla would pull through. It wouldn't be the first time an animal surprised her. Maybe Priscilla hadn't used up her nine lives yet. "Check back with me tomorrow. If she's not better and in pain, we can put her to sleep. She may just go to sleep and not wake up."

"Oh, dear." Mrs. Peterson wiped a tear from her eyes. "She's all we have, Mr. Peterson and I. I don't know what we'd do without her."

"I know." This was one of the worst parts of her profession, when there was nothing she could do. It ranked right up there with putting animals to sleep. It was hard enough when they had lived a long, full life, harder when it was a matter of money, the owner not having enough for expensive treatments. Especially hard when an animal died before its time.

Grace walked Mrs. Peterson to the door then took off her lab coat, exchanged it for her winter coat, and headed out the door. She was late, not that she had an appointment. But she usually made it to the farm before this.

"You're late," Seth stated as she walked to the corral.

"Had a last-minute emergency."

"Sorry to hear that. Did it turn out all right?"

"That's to be seen. What about you? How did it go with your brother? As bad as you expected?"

"Pretty much." Seth shrugged. "Let's focus on happier things, like those horses." Seth nodded in the direction of the horses. They were still in the corral, waiting to be brought in for the night.

"Thank you for not bringing them in yet."

"I knew you wanted to try out what you learned. Let's see what you can do."

Grace flicked on the outdoor lights then entered the corral, her boots sticking in the mud. She wanted to talk to Seth about last night, but figured it could wait. The horses couldn't. They needed to be fed and bedded down for the night. But what was it about those Barton boys? Why didn't they get along?

She decided to work with Lady first, even though that meant working around Peanut who did not leave her side. Eleanor could be cantankerous. She guessed she would be too if she had twins fighting for space in her uterus.

What had seemed so easy under McAdams' instruction seemed impossible now. Had she forgotten already?

"Try having her go around the pen." Seth returned from taking the other mare to her stall.

Grace tried but that had been a round pen. Here there were corners for Lady to hide in, refusing to move. Grace tried to lead her out of the corner and get her to run.

"Maybe she's too tired," Seth suggested.

"Maybe." Lady had been outside all day. At sixteen, she still had a lot of years left, but she definitely wasn't young anymore. Maybe she could use Lady's age to her advantage. Grace decided to lead her into the middle of the corral. Lady resisted. Grace clucked to encourage her to run. Lady didn't run, but she did move out of the corner.

Grace got Lady to follow her, Peanut still at her side, then had her stand while she rubbed her nose and let Lady get to know her again, as if for the first time. Sure, she had examined Lady before, but this was different. That had been as a vet. This was as a trainer and friend. There was a different feel to it.

Grace decided to see if she could get Lady to back up for her. She moved away. Lady followed after her. Grace made sure Lady kept a certain distance.

"You have to gain your horse's respect," Grace remembered McAdams saying. "Don't be so friendly that they forget who's in charge." Then Grace moved towards Lady. Lady moved back easily, as if she had been doing it all her life.

Grace looked over at Seth and smiled. "She did it."

"You did it."

"So that's what I paid all that money for you two to go gallivanting across the country. Of course the horse can do it. She's a trained thoroughbred." Seth's grandfather was standing behind him.

"Gramps, are you sure you're strong enough to be out here?"

"I'm more than strong enough. I'm sick and tired of being cooped up in that house. A little fresh air will do me good. Now show me what you learned at that horse class. And how come you aren't in there working with that mare?" Lamar said to his grandson.

"Because Grace is a natural. She's a born horse whisperer."

"Horse whisperer. That's nonsense. Nothing that a whip and a rope can't do. That's how we trained horses when I was young. That's how these horses were trained."

"How do you know, Gramps?"

"Because that's how it's done."

"Not any more. There are different training techniques. Remember, I told you about them?"

"You talked me into paying your way and this young lady's way to learn about handling horses. Now show me what you learned."

Grace had slipped up next to Lady, allowing her to nuzzle her neck. She had made a start. She was forging a new relationship with this horse. She didn't know how Lady had been trained, but she suspected Seth's grandfather was right. Lady was gentle enough, but she could tell her trainer hadn't been gentle with her. Grace had so much to learn, and Lady had to unlearn some of the habits she had developed over the years. They could learn together. Eleanor, too.

"I think Lady's tired. She's already had a full day. I'll be able to do more on the weekend, when she's fresh from a night of sleep."

"Tired? Babying that horse is what you're doing. But …" Lamar swung his hand in dismissal. "What the heck. I'm not going to breed her again. I might as well let you do what you want."

"You'll be surprised what she can still do." Grace was surprised at the strength with which the words slipped out. "Wait and see."

"I'm sure I will, foolish kids," he muttered and turned to go back to the house.

"Mr. Blackburn," Grace called after him.

"What now?" He turned around.

"It would be helpful if I knew more about her, and Eleanor too. Would help me with training."

"You know about as much as I do."

"Don't you have any papers?"

"You take me for a fool? Of course, I have papers. Wouldn't buy a horse without them. But they don't tell much."

"I'd still like to see them."

"When I dig them out." Lamar headed back to the house.

"I think you're working magic on my grandfather. You got more out of him in this short amount of time than I've gotten out of him after years."

"Well, we'll see," Grace commented. "Let's get these horses fed." She wasn't done with Mr. Blackburn, or his grandsons. Not by a long shot, to use race terminology.

Chapter 13

Grace worked with the two horses after leaving the clinic each night, coming home after supper. Then at night she would go over the training videos or read the book.

"Must be whatever you learned at that horse clinic has had an impact on you. We see you even less than when you were in vet school," her dad commented while she was in the kitchen warming her dinner.

"Sorry, Dad. I don't mean to ignore you. It's just there's so much for me to learn."

"It wouldn't have anything to do with that young man, would it?"

"No, er, not really. He is part of it, but it's really about the horses."

"Tell me about it."

"It's just, while I was there at the horse clinic … I know this will sound funny, but it was as if Mom was there. I felt her presence. Do you think that's possible?" Grace looked across the table at her father, her eyes wide and questioning.

"Of course. I still feel your mom's presence now and then, even though I love Ava."

"What's up?" As if she had been called, Ava joined them in the kitchen. "You two look guilty, like you're plotting something."

Dale smiled and squeezed her hand when she sat down. "Grace was just telling me about the horse clinic."

"Tell me, too."

Grace sat down at the table. Her dad and stepmom sat across from her. "There's not much to tell, just that the trainer — he had me join him in the circle. He showed me a few basic steps."

"That's great," her dad said.

Grace looked over at her stepmom before continuing. "It was like a dance. The trainer talked about it as a dance."

"I've seen some of those dancing horses. They're beautiful," Ava said.

"This was different. It wasn't like that. It was that everything, every movement, was a dance. When I got the horse to step forward and back with me, it was a dance." Grace took a bite of meatloaf before continuing. "All those years at Mom's dance studio. I was never any good at it. I was always clumsy, and … graceless."

"That was just your brother saying that," Ava stated.

"But I was graceless. I never really got it. But now, it's like, I can dance with horses. It's like, I can dance after all. I feel my mom with me when I dance with horses. I know it sounds crazy. I never really knew my mom. I just know I want to learn more, get better at it."

Ava looked away when Grace mentioned her mom. There was that sadness again.

"I don't want you to be sad." Grace reached for Ava's hand.

"I'm not sad." Ava shook her head. "I'm happy for you, that you found a way to connect with your mom." Ava removed her hand from under Grace's, stood up and excused herself. "I've got papers to grade."

"I'm sorry, Dad. I didn't mean to hurt Ava." Grace turned to face her dad once Ava was gone.

"You didn't. Ava meant it, what she said about your mom. This is just something she needs to work out."

"Still, I'm sorry."

"Don't you ever be sorry for doing something you love. Your mom wouldn't want that, nor would Ava. And more importantly, I wouldn't. If you love this so much, God must be in it. Go for it."

God was in it? Grace hadn't thought about that. Was this just a fluke, a passing fancy, or was it God?

Chapter 14

Grace led Lady to her stall after working with her that Saturday, giving the horse a pat before reaching for her curry brush.

"You've been working too hard. Go out with me tonight." Seth slipped up behind her and put his arm around her waist and squeezed.

"Who's going to take care of the horses?"

"I am." Seth took the brush out of her hand. "You go home, relax, and I'll pick you up at seven."

"That would be nice." Grace smiled and started toward her car. She was tired but not too tired to go out with Seth. It would be a pleasant break from her routine.

"Maybe we can find a place where we can dance."

"Oh." Grace stopped.

"Something wrong?"

"It's just, I'm not much of a dancer."

"You're kidding, of course. I see how you move with those horses. You're a natural with them. I'm sure you're just as good on the dance floor. Besides, it's not a competition. It's just about fun."

Fun. Yes, dancing could be fun, she reminded herself as she drove home.

They got burgers at Burger Shack, then Seth took her to a bar that had music.

"This was all the music I could find," he apologized as the band pumped out punk rock. "I wanted something better for you. Something more elegant, graceful, as befitting your name." Seth grabbed a Keno slip, entered some numbers and handed it to their waitress along with some cash. "Maybe this will be our lucky night. Drinks paid for by the state of Michigan."

"This is fine," she said, though she did find the music loud and annoying after a while. She didn't recognize any of the songs.

"All their own music," Seth shouted above the noise. He had talked to some of the band members on his way to the bar to cash in his Keno winnings.

"Not the best for dancing."

"Or listening. Let's go." Seth escorted her out. "Sorry. I'll do better next time," he said as he walked her to the car.

"So, there'll be a next time?"

"Definitely." Seth leaned over and kissed her. "I guess I better get you home. Don't want to get on your dad's bad side."

"I've stayed out later than this."

"I know, with me. I don't want to give your dad the wrong idea, or you either."

"And what idea would that be?"

"That I'm a player."

"Funny. I did think that. Aren't you a player? All those places you've traveled, all the women?" Grace tilted her head and raised her eyebrows as she teased.

"Okay. I can be a player, but not with you."

"Why not?"

Seth's face became serious as he stopped his usual banter. "Because you're the real deal. I don't want to mess it up the way I did with other women." He leaned over and gave her a long slow kiss before starting his car. They drove to her home in silence.

"Why so quiet? I hope I didn't do anything wrong," Seth said as he pulled into her driveway.

"No, not at all. It was sweet."

"Only because you make me sweet."

Grace laughed. "Now that was over the top, even for you, don't you think?"

"I guess I was pouring it on a little thick."

"A little?"

"Okay, a lot. But I do mean it. It's different with you." He leaned over and kissed her again. "I want to do right by you."

Grace slipped out of his car, walked up to her front porch and waved at him before going in. She didn't know why, but something was off. He said all the right things but something didn't strike her as true.

Chapter 15

Grace enlisted Seth's help in getting the horses' papers from his grandfather. His grandfather had been right. Didn't tell much. Still, with the papers and the tattoos in the horses' mouths, she had something to go by.

So much to learn. Thoroughbreds have tattoos. How did they do that? She couldn't imagine a colt or filly holding still for a tattoo. Did that mean they would have to do that to Peanut? It was hard enough to pry Eleanor's and Lady's mouths open to find the tattoo and take a quick photo with her phone.

In a moment of craziness, she had gotten a tattoo on her ankle. She had been with three other pre-vet students after a particularly difficult final exam. They had a few drinks, something uncharacteristic of her, then decided to get tattoos, even more uncharacteristic. She had wanted to get an animal, as befitting a pre-vet student, but opted for a simple flower, a calla lily. Something that didn't require extensive prodding with electrodes. Calla lilies were her mom's favorite flower, or so she had been told.

When Grace shared the tat, she saw that familiar sad look in her stepmother's eyes. Josie had been horrified.

"Why would you inflict pain on your body?"

"But look how pretty it is." Grace showed Josie with her phone.

Maybe Josie was right. She didn't know about physical pain, not the way Josie did. Josie had lived with chronic pain from CMT — Charcout-Marie-Tooth Disorder — a neurological disorder, most of her life. Grace had lived a veritable pain-free existence in comparison, but then there are other pains, hidden pains.

The pain she felt while getting the tattoo was a small semblance of a greater pain, the pain of having lost her mother. She knew some people cut themselves. Was that why? An outward manifestation of inner pain? Or so she justified the tattoo. Why couldn't she enjoy it? A moment of craziness and rebellion in her zipped up, neat life. She didn't do crazy but that one time. She thought about the tat hidden behind her socks in sensible shoes or boots befitting a veterinarian. Even if no one else saw it, knowing it was there helped her feel a little wild, like a feral animal.

The tattoos helped her find Lady's and Eleanor's history. The tats revealed secrets about them, much as her tattoo revealed something about her. Both horses had run in races. Only Lady had placed in any of them. Second and third places. No big wins so her owner was ready to retire her from racing to breed her after two years. When Eleanor didn't place, she was retired after one year. Both had good blood lines. Their foals commanded good prices. Some had gone on to race competitively and done well. Now that they were nearing the end of their breeding years, their owners had been willing to sell them, not cheap. Lamar Blackburn never did anything on the cheap (except for maybe not bringing in a vet for a pregnant mare) but far less than they brought during their peak years.

Grace hoped this wouldn't be Eleanor's last year, not only of foaling, but living. So far there were no problems, but delivering full-term twins, if they made it that long, could be a challenge. Lamar had made his opinion known. If there were problems, she was to save the foals. Clearly the babies Eleanor bore had more value to him than the mare did.

Grace didn't share that sentiment. Seth knew that. How he felt about the situation she wasn't sure. He was beholden to his grandfather. Grace could tell that. How beholden, she wasn't sure. Sometimes it seemed the old man had a hold over him. She didn't understand it, just as she didn't understand his relationship with his brother, Abel. How little she knew about men. Animals were so much easier to understand. More straightforward. No hidden agendas.

Her dad and brother were different from this trio of men. Sure, Jacob picked on her mercilessly as a child, but she always knew he was on her side. And her dad … who didn't love him? He was firm when he needed to be firm. She had seen that with Jacob and Ashley. But never with her.

"I didn't need to be with you," he had explained when she asked him about it. "You always were the easiest of the three. You caused so little grief."

Maybe that was because she saw how much grief Ashley had caused when she moved out, or her dad's frustration and disappointment over Jacob's stunts.

"You were such a joy to your mother and me, still are."

It was a burden to carry, making up to everyone for her birth, being the good child while Ashley and Jacob acted out. Sometimes it was more than she could bear. Hence, a tattoo. A small reminder that she could rebel too, though just a small one. Neither her dad or Ava had reacted.

"Cute," was all her dad had said. Ava hadn't said anything. Just looked away like Grace had disappointed her in some way. That was worse than anger.

Chapter 16

"You ready to ride?" Julia tapped Grace on the shoulder. She and Caroline had come over the following Saturday to ride the mares.

"I don't ride. I'm just the vet."

"Time for that to change. No one sits out when I'm teaching." Julia cinched the saddle. "Western? Is she used to this saddle?"

"I don't know. That's the saddle we have for her. Why?"

"Thoroughbreds don't usually wear Western saddles, though they can. It seems to fit her. Having the right saddle is like having the right shoes. Has she been ridden in open fields before?"

"Not that I know, but I don't know what her previous owners did."

"We'll be careful and test it out before we ride too far." Julia helped Caroline onto Eleanor. "You, up!" She directed Grace to Lady.

"No, I really don't feel ready to ride."

"Okay." Julia gave Caroline some basic instructions, then stood next to Lady and rubbed her nose and side body while Caroline walked Eleanor around the corral. "We aren't going to ride you hard, Mama. Understand?"

The horse nodded as if she understood what Julia had said. Julia checked the saddle, made sure it fit properly, then lightly lifted herself onto the horse. "You sure you don't want to try?" she asked Grace again.

Grace shook her head. A definite no.

"Think about it. We'll take a short ride then it will be your turn. Besides, can't work the new mama too hard with her colt still following her around. We have to make sure her baby can keep up." Julia clucked to the mare and led Caroline out of the corral and into the pasture.

Grace watched Eleanor canter around the pasture area. Caroline appeared to be learning quickly.

"Your turn," Julia insisted as they rode the horses back into the corral.

"No, I can't …" Grace resisted.

"Of course you can. You're a natural," Seth urged her on. "I'll show you."

"I thought you didn't ride."

"Did I ever say that?"

"No, not really. I guess I just assumed so when you didn't."

"You assume too much. Do you really think I could have lived here all those years in my teens and not learned how to ride a horse?"

"I guess I didn't think. I did wonder. Then why haven't you ridden them?"

"Didn't have a reason to. Besides, I was never that good. Abel, now Abel, he was the real rider."

"Then why didn't he ride when he was here?"

Seth shrugged and hopped on Lady. "People change."

Julia helped Grace onto Eleanor. "Remember what I told Caroline?"

"I think I do."

"Don't worry. Eleanor already knows and trusts you. Listen to her. She'll take you where you need to go." Julia patted Eleanor on the rump as Grace walked her around the corral a few times, getting the feel of the reins and how to direct Eleanor which way to turn. It was different from being on the ground leading, and yet the same. It just took a little adjustment on her part.

Seth took Lady out at a trot, being careful to watch for the colt. Grace took a deep breath and followed after him as Julia and Caroline watched. Her body bounced at the rough pace, like she was being shaken.

"Loosen up." Seth rode up to her. "You're tight. Relax. Let your body move with the horse."

Grace tightened up even more, her hand clutching the horn of the saddle. She wanted down. Yet another thing she wasn't good at. As if in response to her unspoken words, Eleanor stopped and began to graze.

"Relax, Grace." Seth came over next to her and reached for Eleanor's reins. "You trust me, don't you?"

"No." Grace shook her head. "I don't trust you. I don't trust myself. I want to go back to the corral." Tears stung her eyes. Here she thought she would hop on and be transformed. She would be one with the horse. She would take the dance she had been learning to a new level. Instead she was just as awkward and unsure as she was in the dance studio. She had fooled herself into thinking this would be different.

Eleanor balked under her direction. She could tell Grace was uncertain. She refused to go any further, instead chomping on the remnants of grass in the pasture. Seth let go of the reins as Grace tried to pull Eleanor's head back up. Eleanor raised her head, turned and headed back to the corral at a canter. Grace was happy to let Eleanor take the lead, though she would have preferred a slower pace.

Julia and Caroline were waiting for them at the corral.

"That wasn't bad for a first time," Julia told her.

"No, it was terrible. Eleanor knew I didn't know what I was doing. She knew who was in charge and it wasn't me."

"That's okay. You'll do better next time. Eleanor was tired. Next time you ride Lady, or ride Eleanor first, before she gets tired. Once a horse gets turned toward home, it's hard to keep them from heading there, especially if they are tired." Julia held Eleanor while Grace dismounted. "You just need to be more confident."

Grace's legs shook underneath her as she adjusted to being on solid ground. There won't be a next time. She didn't have to ride horses to treat them as a vet. Why put herself through this again? Ashley and Jacob, they were the athletes. They had inherited their mom's ability. She was just Graceless, like Jacob always called her. Might as well accept it.

Seth joined her. "You did fine for your first time. My first time riding I didn't even get out of the corral. You need more confidence."

"I'm confident I won't do this again."

"Why? You're a horse person. Why miss out on the fun of riding?"

"Because I'm happiest with my two feet on the ground."

"Thanks for letting us ride." Julia hugged Grace then took Eleanor's reins from her. "Part of learning how to ride is taking care of your horse afterwards. Caroline and I will brush them down. It will give you two a break."

Grace started to protest when Julia put her hand on her shoulder. "Let us do this. It's good for Caroline." They climbed back up and walked the two mares around the corral to let them cool down though neither had been ridden hard. Then they tied them to the hitching post and brought over buckets of water.

Grace and Seth showed them where to place the gear and where to find the grooming supplies for the horses. Caroline was a natural. She was fearless as she brushed Lady down, rubbing the curry comb in circular motions around her body, then using different brushes to get rid of any dirt as well as cleaning her hooves. Another reminder to Grace of her inadequacies. Even this fourteen-year-old girl was better at riding horses than she was. She'd stick to her vet work. It was what she was good at.

"There's a lot of work involved with taking care of horses," Caroline said when she rejoined Grace and Seth.

"I told you it wasn't just about riding," her mom said. "If you are going to ride horses, you need to know how to care for them as well. You still want to ride?"

"More than ever." Caroline looked from her mother to Grace and Seth. "Do you think I could come over and ride sometimes after school? I could help take care of the horses. Clean their stalls."

"That's up to your mom and Seth," Grace said. She had been younger than Caroline when she had started volunteering at the vet clinic. Maybe if she had started riding horses back then she would have mastered it by now. But that was then. Now was too late.

"Sure," Seth said. "As long as it's okay with your mom. I could use the help mucking out the stalls. Not my favorite job. Though I think you need more lessons, riding under your mother's instruction before riding alone."

"How will you get here?" Julia asked.

"I can be dropped off by the bus. Then Grace could bring me home when she comes."

"We'll talk about it," Julia told her. "Thank you, Grace." Julia hugged her again as she said goodbye, squeezing her tight as if pouring confidence into her.

Grace waved as they drove away.

"So, we going out tonight?" Seth asked.

Grace wanted to say no. She wanted to sulk in a bath of melancholy on yet another failure to live up to the legacy of her siblings.

"You aren't going to let that little problem with Eleanor put you into a funk, are you? I won't let you go home and sulk."

Grace smiled. "When you put it that way, how can I say no?" Having a boyfriend meant having a regular Saturday night date. This was new for her. She couldn't always do what she wanted to do. She kind of liked it.

True to her word, Grace continued to refuse to ride the mares each time Julia came over with Caroline. She dug in her heels, not budging. She rarely did this, but when she did, there was no moving her. She was every bit as stubborn as Eleanor when she had enough and refused to go further. When working with Eleanor in the corral, Grace had learned to listen to what Eleanor was telling her when she did this.

"Okay. Are you calling it a day? I guess I would be tired too if I was carrying twins." Then she would cradle Eleanor's head and let her nuzzle until she was ready to move again. "You have to make allowances for pregnant mares," she told herself.

Caroline worked out an agreement with her mother where she would ride the bus to Blackburn farm twice a week.

"As long as she keeps up with her homework," Julia insisted. Caroline cleaned the stalls and brushed the mares. Grace taught her what little she knew about horses. She could see Caroline would surpass her soon. On the weekends when Julia was available, she gave Caroline riding instructions.

"Soon Caroline will have learned all I have to teach her," Julia said to Grace as they both watched. "I guess I'll have to look for a riding instructor." Julia continued to watch her daughter, not looking at Grace as she said, "You sure you don't want to give it another try?"

"I'm sure."

"Maybe when that horse whisperer comes. What's his name, McAdams? Maybe he'll change your mind." Brody was scheduled to come that April for a clinic. Grace cringed internally at the thought. How embarrassing if he knew.

"We'll see," Grace said. Not likely, she added to herself.

Chapter 17

They had a policy at the clinic, restrictive collars with "pinchers" were removed while your pet was in the exam room. This was to create a warm and welcoming environment for the pet. Most of the time Grace agreed with this policy, but there were days …

Like the Labrador puppy that slipped out of his owner's embrace, raced in between the vet tech's legs as the tech was opening the door and raced through the hallway and into the waiting room, knocking over carts, terrorizing kittens, being hissed at by cats and picking a fight with a boxer — all in good fun. You would think with the limited space they had, he would have quickly been caught and corralled into submission. It's amazing how much damage a determined animal can do in a short span of time.

Or the mastiff who broke loose from his owner and insisted on peeing on Grace's leg, the waiting room carpet and potted flowers. Or the cat who jumped off her owner's lap in pursuit of a pet gerbil. How do you spell lunch if you are a cat? Precisely. And of course, the occasional animal that nips at you when you examine their teeth or stick something up their rear. And the dog that escapes out the front door and into the parking lot.

Better yet were the stories their owners told. She remembered the stories Ashley and Jacob used to tell about Lucky, their first family dog. How he had knocked the spaghetti onto the kitchen floor and how Grandma Esther had chased him. Grace had been a baby when Lucky first found them. She didn't remember that adventure. That had been when her mom had relapsed and was back at the hospital. Seems Lucky had found them just when they needed him most. She knew the story from the retelling, each time with an embellishment. She had memories of her own as over time Lucky had gone from being

Ashley's dog to her dog. Grace had only been ten when Lucky died, but she remembered how Ashley, Jacob and she had spent the night with him, sleeping in the living room in order to be with him at the end.

It had been a peaceful death, without any medical intervention. A natural death after a long life. She judged every other death against this gold standard. Most often they fell short, not because animals didn't die naturally, but because you didn't need a vet in those situations.

"Ms. Anderson and Ms. Jones are here," her receptionist interrupted her thought process. Her second appointment for the day. The two women, Anne Anderson and Erin Jones, were bringing in their precious cat today for her final journey. She didn't know them that well. Didn't need to. All she needed to do was care for their pet. Some people judged the two women harshly. She didn't understand why. Why can't we all just get along, live in peace? Why can't people just live and let live? The couple quietly lived together. For all she knew they were just friends. No displays of affection. She wondered how they had found each other. They were as devoted to that cat as any couple she saw at the clinic. They had waited until both could take time off of work to be there at the end. Grace tried to be as unobtrusive as possible, not wanting to invade their privacy as they shared their grief.

Anne held the cat as Grace administered the lethal dose. Erin looked away, unable to watch. Grace waited till she knew the drug had done its job, then slipped out of the room to leave them alone together.

It was a privilege to be there. She saw brusque, burly men tear up at the loss of a beloved pet, stoic mothers break down while their children watched, more at peace with the process than their parent.

"It's okay, Mama," one brave girl said after the loss of their dog. "Suzy's in a better place, like you told us."

A better place? Did she believe that? There's no mention in the Bible of animals going to Heaven. If they didn't go to Heaven, where did they go? She didn't know. What she did know was that they had a spirit. She had seen it, heard it, felt it, even smelled it. A smell like no other. She had no words to describe it.

Other animals knew when one of their kind passed away. She remembered one night while on call. She had been called to care for a dog who had been hit by a car. The dog was too injured to move so she had gone to the home and found the animal wrapped in a blanket in the living room while the children gathered around him. It reminded her of Lucky.

A farm family, they had two other dogs and several cats, as well as farm animals. The dogs were keeping vigil in the mud room when she arrived. She tended his wounds, did what she could, but feared the worse. She suspected he had internal injuries.

"If he makes it through the night, bring him to the clinic tomorrow for x-rays," she said as the farmer escorted her out past the sad dogs in the mud room.

Grace paused when she reached her car and looked back at the house. The dogs in the mud room began to howl and the barn animals mooed, brayed and oinked in farewell. Grace looked up at the chimney and saw a wisp of smoke floating out into the star filled sky. She didn't need to call the next day to confirm what she already knew.

Animals had a soul. That she knew. Where they went, she didn't know. Even Pastor Joe didn't know. He had stuttered back when she had first asked him after Lucky had died.

"What do you think?"

Grace knew this trick. Pastor Joe always turned the question back on to her. She figured it meant he didn't know.

"I think Lucky's in Heaven, along with all of the other pets who were loved during their lifetime."

"Then I think you have your answer."

It had gotten Pastor Joe off the hook at the time, but the answer failed to satisfy her as she grew older. She wanted to know more.

She read that Native Americans believed people had spirit animals. They would go out on a quest when they were teens to discover their spirit animal. She wondered what her spirit animal was. Maybe it was Lucky? Maybe beloved animals came back as spirit animals?

But that didn't satisfy her either. What would Heaven be without animals? She couldn't imagine. You were supposed to be perfectly happy in Heaven. She didn't see how she could be happy if there were no animals.

"I'm sure that God has it worked out," her grandmother said when Grace asked her. After all, Grandma knew more about Heaven than just about anyone else she knew. She was so close to Heaven herself, being eighty and knowing so many people there. More than Grace knew. If Grandma believed animals were in Heaven, that was enough for her.

Grace examined the litter of puppies that had been brought in for their check up and shots. All healthy. Some die, others are born. That's how it goes. You grieve the loss but new life required you to go on. Someone had to care for the young. Someone had to care for the animals. It gave her reason to keep going when confused and frustrated by life.

Chapter 18

Christmas was almost here. This would be her first Christmas with a boyfriend. Did she dare invite Seth to her family Christmas celebrations? How could she celebrate Christmas without him? There was the Christmas Eve Service, followed by dinner and presents. Then Christmas dinner the next day. That was a lot to ask of anybody. And what of his own family? How was she to be involved? Relationships are complicated.

"I would love to have a real Christmas with a real family," Seth had said when she broached the possibility during their weekly Saturday evening date. "Only Gramps expects me for Christmas dinner."

"He can come with you. What's one more person? My family is always ready to welcome guests."

"And then there's Abel."

"He can come too."

"You don't get it."

"Then explain it to me. Wouldn't they enjoy a great meal with an exceptional family? Who wouldn't? We know how to do Christmas." How could anyone say no to such an invite? Grace squeezed his arm while they walked back to his car.

"And not be able to grouse and complain? That wouldn't be a Blackburn Christmas. It wouldn't be Christmas without a family blow-up."

"It will be a great Christmas. You'll see. Invite them."

"I'll mention it to Gramps, but don't expect much." Seth opened the car door for her and waited for her to climb in.

Grace recognized that tone of voice. It wasn't going to happen. "Then, do you want me to come to your grandfather's for Christmas dinner?" she asked once he was seated in the driver's side of the car.

"I wouldn't want to put you through that."

"How bad could it be?"

"Bad. I'll see."

Grace was relieved when she didn't have to go to Christmas dinner at the Blackburn farm. She didn't like conflict, so she suspected she wouldn't like dinner with the Blackburns. But she had been willing. You do these things when you have a boyfriend. She had a boyfriend.

"You will be able to come over on Christmas Eve, won't you?" Grace asked.

"No. I'm sorry, Grace. But Gramps would like you to stop over for a drink. You could stop after church."

And miss out on her family's Christmas Eve fun? Grace bit her lip and turned away from him.

"It won't be long," Seth continued, not waiting for an answer. "Just a drink. And maybe then I could slip away and go to your family's celebration." Seth reached over and took her hand, forcing her to look at him. "You know, I'd much rather be with you, but Gramps, he holds the purse strings. He thinks that gives him the right to run my life."

"When are you going to stand up to him?" Grace challenged him.

"In due time." Seth leaned over and kissed her. "Say you'll come for a drink on Christmas Eve."

"All right." How could she resist? "But then you'll come to my aunt's house, right? No one will believe I have a boyfriend if you don't show up."

"I'll try."

It wasn't everything she wanted, but it was something. Compromise. Isn't that what relationships are about?

Chapter 19

Grace wished Seth had agreed to come to the Christmas Eve service with her. She knew relationships were about compromise, but why was she the one doing all the compromising?

She hadn't pushed church on Seth. They had talked about church and religion.

"I don't have a problem with you attending church. Church and religion are okay for other people."

"Just not you."

"Right. It's not right for me. I'm more of a philosopher. I've studied the great philosophers from Socrates, Plato and the Greeks on through Kant, Descartes and Hegel."

"You do believe in God, don't you?"

"I believe in a supernatural power, a supreme being you might say. But God, especially God as an actual person … Nah."

"You don't believe in Jesus?"

"As a great philosopher, yes. God? No. Is that a problem?"

"I don't know. I guess not," she had said then, but when she had said it, she didn't realize what it meant. Sundays going to church alone. Christmas Eve, Easter … not even being able to share holidays?

"If it's a big deal to you, I'll go, but my grandfather expects me to go to church with him."

"Then you do have some church background."

"Episcopalian, but not much. I only go now and then with Gramps to keep him happy."

Was that what she was doing? Going to church to keep her dad, her family, happy? It was difficult when your uncle was the pastor. There are expectations that come with being related to the pastor.

Church and religion were often the topic of conversation over the Sunday dinner table.

"Try growing up with your father being pastor. Talk about a fishbowl." Stephanie was always quick to comment about how hard she had it growing up as a P.K. – preacher's kid.

"That didn't keep you from doing pretty much whatever you wanted," Gus said.

"What do you know about it?" Stephanie asked.

"I hear things, some at this table." Gus popped a piece of buttered roll into his mouth.

"Your mother was quite the partier in high school." Josh smiled across the table at Gus. "And beyond."

"Are you the one telling Gus stories?" Stephanie's eyes blazed. Grace was uncomfortable when Stephanie looked like that, but it didn't bother Josh.

"I'm not making up anything. Just telling the truth." Josh winked at Stephanie. That served to make her angrier.

"With a little embellishment, no doubt." Peter raised his eyebrows and looked at Josh.

"If anyone is going to talk about living in a fishbowl ..." Aunt Kathleen started. Everyone groaned.

"Come on, Mom. You lived in the manse for maybe one year. That hardly compares to Stephanie who lived there all her childhood," Josh interrupted her.

"You don't have to live in a manse to live in a fish bowl," Aunt Kathleen replied.

"Come on in. The water's fine." Uncle Joe poked Aunt Kathleen.

"It is as long as I'm with you." Aunt Kathleen poked him back then kissed him.

"Aw, really, Mom." Josh rolled his eyes. "How long have you two been married?"

"Not long enough," Aunt Kathleen responded. "I have a lot of missed time to make up for — right, husband?"

"Right, wife." Uncle Joe kissed her back. "Lots of couples our age are celebrating their fortieth anniversary. We're only at fifteen. We have a way to go. That means we have to make every year count."

"That's fifteen years longer than I've been married," Josh said.

"Because no one would have you," Stephanie quipped.

"You're not much better. I don't see any ring on your finger."

"Not because I haven't been asked." Stephanie had been engaged a couple times that Grace was aware of. She didn't know why Stephanie wasn't married.

"I think it's good for young people to see a happy marriage. And I intend to kiss my bride." Peter leaned over and planted a big kiss on Grandma Esther.

Grandma laughed. "If you think that is going to get you an extra piece of pie …"

"Pie?" Grace's dad asked. "Count me in on this. I'm kissing my bride, too."

Ava stood up before he could reach her. "If you want a kiss, you'll have to help me in the kitchen."

"Gladly." Her dad winked and followed Ava into the kitchen. "Kissing in the kitchen."

It was a fish bowl, being a part of the pastor's family, even if he was just her uncle. Being a part of this family. Being a part of the church family. It was a fish bowl, but Uncle Joe was right. The water wasn't bad.

She thought about this as she sat in the darkened church, held her lit candle and sang Silent Night. She wished Seth were here to share this with her. Maybe another time. She looked around the full church, faces of extended family and friends hardly recognizable in the shadows.

"I won't be too late," Grace told her grandma and Aunt Kathleen after the service. "Don't wait for me. I'll be over as soon as I can."

"And bring that young man with you," Grandma said. "It's about time I met him."

"You sure he's ready to meet us?" Aunt Kathleen asked.

"The sooner I get out of here, the sooner I'll be able to make it over." Grace ignored Aunt Kathleen's question. She had asked herself the same thing several times over.

Just a quick drink, Seth had assured her. Grace pulled up the familiar drive and parked by the house this time, not the barn. It felt funny, not going to see the horses. Grace had seen them that afternoon. She didn't want to trudge through the snow to the barn and ruin her good boots, the only dress boots she had. Black with short, spiky heels, giving her a few inches of extra height. She pulled her mid-length, red coat about her as she walked to the porch.

She was surprised when Seth wasn't at the door waiting for her. She had texted him that she was there. She knocked on the door and waited, shivering in the cold. She wished she had worn her down coat, but that wouldn't do for Christmas Eve. Wasn't nice enough. When no one answered the door after several raps, she tried the knob. Unlocked. She let herself in.

"Hello?" she called. "Merry Christmas." She walked through the kitchen, past the dining room where the table was set for dinner, to the parlor where she had met Seth's grandfather before. She found the men there. Despite the fire blazing in the fireplace and the Christmas lights that adorned the mantel, the room was chilly, not with cold, but with a chill that cut her heart. Seth's brother Abel was standing by the fire leaning against the mantle, a drink in his hand. The fire and lights cast a glow against his face, leaving it in a shadow, but not the warm shadow she had experienced in the church. His face was unreadable. Seth's grandfather sat in his accustomed chair looking even more cross than he did normally.

It didn't feel like Christmas.

Grace searched the room for Seth.

"Seth told you I was coming, didn't he? I mean, he told me you invited me." Grace looked over at Lamar, waiting for a response.

"You did invite her, right Gramps?" Seth appeared out of the shadow in the corner holding a drink. "I'm sorry, Grace. Through no fault of your own, you have come at a bad time."

"Seth, what's going on? What's wrong?"

"It seems my dear brother here, and my grandfather, have conspired together to send me away. And on Christmas, no less."

"What are you talking about?" Grace looked from one man to the other, settling her gaze on Seth. Surely he would come over, give her a reassuring hug, take her arm, take her coat, invite her to sit down. Instead, Mr. Blackburn broke the silence.

"I'm sorry, dear. It seems there's been a misunderstanding."

"You did invite me, didn't you?"

"Yes, I did. But now, I'm afraid you must go. We have a family matter that must be dealt with."

"But it's Christmas," Grace said.

"It seems this won't wait. Abel, will you see Dr. Reese out?"

Grace looked at Seth, imploring him with her eyes to say something, do something.

Seth turned away from her. "I'm sorry, Grace."

"We'll talk later?" she asked. "You'll call me?" He didn't respond.

Abel left his station at the fireplace and approached her to do his grandfather's bidding. She searched his face. Unreadable. How could this be happening? Just a few minutes ago she had been happy. Now she didn't know what to think.

"Let me show you to the door." Abel reached out a hand to guide her.

"Thank you but I'm perfectly capable of finding my own way out." Grace refused his hand and retreated the same way she had come in. Abel followed her despite what she had said, turning on the outside light of the porch. A light dusting of snow was falling, already covering up the steps she had made on her way in. She started her car, turned on the windshield wiper and glanced up at the dark figure, standing on the porch, waiting for her to leave.

She didn't stop to gather her thoughts. She just drove. She had to get out of there. But what would she tell her family?

Chapter 20

Presents were being passed around when she arrived. She fixed herself a plate of food from the rich array which was Christmas Eve at the Reese's, then settled on a chair close to the entrance to the living room without saying a word. Her grandmother nodded hello and raised an eyebrow, questioning where Seth was without saying a word. Grace gave a slight shrug, then took a bite of the food. Tasteless. The rest of her food remained untouched on her plate. Her grandma didn't say a word. Around her, cheerful conversation and laughter filled the room as presents were given out and opened. Grace didn't hear what was being said until a present was plopped on her lap.

"Open your present, Grace. It's from me." Gus handed her a gift. Each Christmas they drew names for a gift exchange, otherwise they would have been there all-night opening presents. Individual families had their own gift exchange Christmas morning. They always had a few extra gifts wrapped for any guests that might join them. Grace lifted the box and shook it, then made a guess as to its contents as was their tradition.

"Hmmm, socks?" she ventured, pushing herself to get into the spirit.

"Socks wouldn't make that harsh a sound or slide back and forth like that," her dad said, as whatever was inside slid back and forth hitting the sides.

"Underwear?" Grace shook the package again and tilted her head to tease Gus.

"Just open it," Gus told her.

Grace unwrapped the package. Inside was a book on horses, on training and riding them.

"Caroline told me how much you love horses. Do you like it?"

"Of course, I do." But I don't ride, she thought to herself as she hugged Gus. "I love it."

"We have a gift for Seth too," Aunt Kathleen said. "Where is he?"

"Something came up. He couldn't make it," Grace mumbled.

"Here, you give it to him. We heard he was a student of art and philosophy so we got him a book on Leonardo DaVinci." Aunt Kathleen handed Grace the package.

"Thank you. I'm sure Seth will love it."

"When do we meet this mystery man?" Stephanie asked. "He has to pass inspection like all of my boyfriends. Have to make sure he's fit to date our Grace."

Ava stepped in. "We've met him and he's a fine young man."

"Not enough. You know the tradition," Stephanie continued.

"I'm sure we'll get to meet him when the time is right," Grandma Esther intervened. "Who's hungry? It's time for round two." At this the adults groaned while the kids and teens raced back to the dining room table to help themselves to another round of snacks, appetizers and desserts.

Scott and Alex left first with their three kids. "Have to get these kids in bed before Santa comes," Scott said.

The rest began to filter out. Grace helped clear the food off the table, joining her grandmother in the kitchen.

"No Seth?"

Grace shook her head.

"That's okay. We can talk about it some other time." Her grandmother gave her a quick squeeze of support. Grandma knew when she wanted to talk and when she didn't without her having to say a word.

"Here." Aunt Kathleen came into the kitchen with the last plate of food. "I'll pack these up so you can take it home with you for tomorrow."

They always had more food than they could eat. The leftovers from tonight would go with the appetizers and desserts for tomorrow's dinner at her home. Then those leftovers would be sent home with guests and family members. Even so, Grace knew she would be eating turkey all week.

Grace left before her parents, hoping to be in bed, if not asleep, when they got home. Seth's car was parked in front of her house when she pulled into the driveway. Seth opened her passenger side door and climbed in.

"Grace, I'm so sorry. Can we talk?"

"Seth, what was that all about? What is going on with your family?"

"I can't explain now. I have to leave."

"Leave? When?"

"Tonight." The word sounded hollow in the small car.

"But it's Christmas." How could this be? How could he leave on Christmas?

"It may be Christmas for you and for the rest of the world, but for the Blackburn family, it's just another day, no different from any other."

"I don't understand." Grace shook her head as if that would clear away all the confusion and give her the clarity she sought.

"I know you don't. I'll explain, some day. But for now, I couldn't leave without giving you your present." Seth handed her a neatly wrapped box tied with ribbon and a bow.

"But …" Grace accepted the gift, looking first at the box, then at him.

"Open it."

Grace felt Seth's eyes on her as she carefully unwrapped the package. She didn't want to rush the moment, wanted to keep him here with her for as long as possible. She lifted the top of the box and pulled back the layer of protective wrapping to reveal a framed picture of two horses, racing to the finish line.

"That's not just any horse," Seth said.

"You mean?"

"Yes, that's Lady. She took second place, but you can see her better than the first-place winner." There was Lady in all her glory, nostrils flaring, eyes bright, pulling up alongside another horse.

"How did you get this?" Grace looked up from the picture into his eyes.

"Once I had her record, it was just a matter of contacting the right people. It wasn't as easy for Eleanor." Seth pointed back at the box.

Grace pulled out another framed picture. There was Eleanor, surrounded by other running horses, but still Grace was able to pick her out.

"Seth, this is …" What could she say?

"It's incredible, isn't it?"

"Yes, it is. You're incredible." She sat with the pictures on her lap, struggling to find the right words.

"You remember that when I'm gone."

"But I don't understand. Why do you have to leave?"

"You can thank my brother Abel for that." There was that dark look she had seen before when Seth talked about his brother.

"What does he have to do with it, with anything?"

"Nothing. I really can't talk about it now. Later, when I get back."

"But when will that be?"

"I don't know, but I will be back. I promise you that."

"Seth, I just, I don't understand." She took his hand as if that would keep him from leaving.

"Understand this. I love you, Grace Reese. You incredible, amazing woman. And someday I'll be back to prove it." He leaned over and kissed her just as Grace's parents pulled into the driveway. "I've got to go. Remember what I said. I'll be back."

How could she forget? No man not related to her had ever told her he loved her before. She'd remember him forever. But why did he have to go? She sat in the car while Seth took off. Her parents pulled past her into the garage.

"But I didn't give him his present." Grace pulled out her phone and texted him.

"I'll get it when I come back." Seth texted back.

When he comes back, not if, she told herself. It was a small comfort.

Chapter 21

Grace didn't know what to do. It was Christmas. She had Christmas breakfast with Dad and Ava, opened the gifts they had for her, then helped prepare Christmas dinner for the whole family while avoiding talking to Ava. If only Josie had come home for Christmas. But Jacob didn't have enough time between games to come home for Christmas and Josie wasn't coming home without him. She was working on her Masters in Environmental Science and saving the world while Jacob played pro basketball with the Golden State Warriors.

"Why don't you come spend Christmas with us?" Josie had asked like she did every year. Grace gave her the same answer she gave every year.

"Can't. I can't take time off from the clinic."

"Is it that you can't take the time, or you won't take the time? Or does this have something to do with that man you've been seeing?"

Josie was the person she wanted to talk to. If only she had gone to California for Christmas, she could have avoided all this drama. But then Seth would have been gone without a goodbye. When things quieted down, when family was gone and Christmas over, later that night, she would call Josie.

But what about Lady, Eleanor and Peanut? What was she to do? Who would take care of them now that Seth was gone? Certainly not Abel. She had to go to the farm and make sure they were okay first, then she would call Josie.

Grace helped with the dishes and clean-up. A few stragglers were still there, including Grandma Esther, Peter, Aunt Kathleen, Uncle Joe and Gus, when she excused herself.

"Don't you get a day off?" Aunt Kathleen asked.

"Horses need to eat just like people," Grace said as she left.

Grace pulled down the long driveway and parked by the barn, as far from the house as she could. She didn't want to be seen by anyone from the house, though her car was clearly visible as it made its way down the driveway.

The horses were out in the corral. That was good. At least they were getting some exercise and not cooped up in their stalls all day. She checked and saw they had water. Abel must have taken care of that. All she needed to do was bring them in and feed them.

"I didn't think you would come after what happened last night."

Grace jumped at the deep voice. Abel. He had a heavy flannel coat thrown on over jeans and a shirt. Nothing like the business man she had seen last night and before at the clinic.

"I'm still their vet. I have to make sure they are cared for, especially Eleanor."

"Thank you."

"I'm not doing it for you. I'm doing it for the horses."

"Then thank you from them." He moved closer and put his hand on her arm. "I'm glad you're here. I need to talk to you."

Grace pulled away. "Then talk."

"About the horses. My grandfather is okay on his own with his housekeeper, but he can't take care of the horses. The girl who has been helping out."

"Caroline."

"Yes, Caroline. I'd like to pay her to look after the horses, feed them, brush them down, clean their stalls. Do you have her contact information?"

"I do, but she's in high school. Can't even drive yet. I don't know if she'll be able to come every day."

"Would you be able to help on the days she can't? I'll pay you."

She looked at the man who had destroyed her future, sent the man she loved away. She hated him. She didn't want to do anything for him, didn't want anything to do with him.

"Don't do it for me, do it for the horses, and for my grandfather. You don't hate him, do you?"

Grace shook her head. No, she didn't hate him, but she didn't know what part Lamar Blackburn played in sending away his grandson. She didn't know what to say.

"Twins are a high-risk pregnancy." Grace refused to look at him. She turned away and focused on the horses.

"I'm aware of that."

"I need to keep checking on Eleanor and when she gets closer to foaling, someone will have to keep an eye on her to make sure she doesn't go off by herself to have the babies. Even if delivered safely, the foals will need extra care and attention until they are strong enough to survive." Grace continued to look at the horses.

"That's what I'll be paying you for."

"You think that money solves every problem?" She turned to confront him.

"It's solved any problem I've encountered."

"You can't buy me. I'll take care of Eleanor and the other horses. I'll stay with her till the twins are born and help with the foals until they are strong enough to get by, but after that I'll be gone. You'll have to find someone else to take care of them and clean up your mess." She hoped her voice sufficiently expressed her disdain for him.

"That's more than I hoped for. By then, I'll have other arrangements, or maybe my grandfather will finally come to his senses and realize he's too old to take care of horses."

Grace gulped. Was he talking about selling the horses? It was bad enough he had sent Seth away. Now he was going to send her horses away too? Her chest hurt. A heaviness expanded under her ribs and she couldn't catch her breath. She didn't know which hurt worse: Seth being gone, or the possibility of losing the horses.

"You okay?" Grace ignored the care in his voice. He was not to be trusted.

"I'm fine, just fine. Not that you care. I just need to catch my breath." Grace tried to take a deep breath. Nothing that a good cry wouldn't solve but she wouldn't give him the satisfaction of seeing her cry.

"Maybe you should come into the house and have some water."

"I told you, I'm fine. Now, if you'll let me do my job." Why doesn't he leave? Let her be so she can treat herself to a pity party?

"It's Christmas. I can take care of the horses today, but I have to leave tomorrow. If you could come back then, I'd appreciate it. And I need the contact information for Caroline."

"I'll call and give you the number when I get home."

"Here." Abel reached into his back pocket and pulled a business card out of his wallet. He pulled a pen out of his coat pocket, removed his gloves and fumbled to write on the back of the card, his fingers turning blue from the cold.

"You certainly are prepared."

"It's business. Always have to be prepared." He handed her the card. "Here's my business card. My personal cell phone number is on the back. Call that number any time. I want to know if there are any problems, especially with my grandfather. You'd be doing me a great personal favor if you could check on him from time to time."

Could there be a heart in that expansive chest? Not possible.

"I'll check on him, but not for you. For Seth. Seth would want to know if there's anything wrong with his grandfather. He would be happy to know I'm looking out for him."

"I don't care why you do it, just so you do it."

Grace took the card and slipped it in her coat pocket and walked to her car. Her anger gave her strength. Plenty enough time to collapse once she was safely home.

Chapter 22

She sat in the driveway and cried once she got home. That was where Ava found her. Ava hugged her and insisted she come inside. Then she pampered her, bringing her cocoa and Christmas cookies, hugging her and letting her cry until she was ready to be done.

"As far as I'm concerned, neither of those Blackburn boys are worthy of you," Ava came to her rescue without being asked.

There were good things about living at home, but the person she really needed to talk to was Josie.

"Sounds to me like that is not a family you want to be part of," Josie said when she told her what had happened. "You don't just marry the man. You marry the family. Can you imagine spending holidays year after year with that family? Do you really want that? I'm lucky. I already know and love Jacob's family."

"Listen to you, all full of words of wisdom. Since when have you become the love guru?"

"I'm not. I'm just sharing some of my experience. It also almost sounds like it would have been harder for you to leave the horses than Seth," Josie suggested.

"No, of course not," Grace insisted. But was Josie right? Josie knew her better than anyone.

"I'm just saying what I'm hearing. It sounds to me like you are more upset over the possibility of the horses being sold than Seth being gone."

"They are connected."

"Then that's not good. Do you love Seth because of the horses and the time you spend together taking care of them, or do you love him for himself? It takes more than common interests to make a relationship work."

Josie did know something about relationships now that she and Jacob were together. She still wondered what Josie saw in her brother. He was her brother. She loved him but she knew his faults far too well. They had so little in common. What was the glue that held them together?

"You don't know your brother the way I do. He can be very sweet and caring."

Grace knew that. She knew he had a good side. He also had a wild side.

"And he has settled down," Josie added.

"If he has, it's because you're a good influence on him."

"That I am, but we were talking about you, not me."

Yes, they had been talking about her, but she'd much rather talk about Josie, or anything or anybody besides herself.

"If I had known Seth was going to leave, I would have made arrangements to fly out to San Francisco and see you." Except for pets being boarded over the Christmas holidays, the clinic was closed between Christmas and New Year's. They had staff looking in on the animals, feeding them and taking them outside. That didn't require her.

"It's not too late. We'll pay for your ticket."

"No, I have to take care of the horses and I'd have to arrange for someone to take my on-call hours. Better off this way." She didn't really want to go. It required too much effort and would have interfered with her feeling sorry for herself.

Without the daily structure of work, she found herself lying in bed late, moping around. Only Ava had a different idea. She was home all week because of school being out. Ava had been sympathetic on Christmas night but wasn't one to let her mope. "It's not that I don't love having you around, it's just — are you sure you're okay? Don't you have somewhere to go? Something to do?"

Maybe staying around the house wasn't the best idea. The only thing she had to get her out of the house were the horses at Blackburn farm and the need to take care of them.

Grace was surprised to see a familiar car at the farm when she pulled up. Not Julia's car, but Henry's car, Caroline's father.

Grace found Caroline in the barn mucking out a stall.

"Where's your dad?" she asked.

"He's up at the house, talking to Mr. Blackburn. Dad said he's done business with him in the past, said he'd keep him company while I worked." Henry was a local lawyer and a respected one. As such he knew pretty much everyone in Cascade Falls. "Isn't it great? Dad doesn't work this week so he said he would drive me here every day so I can do my chores. Why are you here?"

"Just checking on the horses."

"Mr. Blackburn's grandson, Abel, is paying me to take care of the horses. You will be able to drive me home on school nights when I take the bus here, won't you?"

"I didn't think your mom was going to let you come every day?"

"That was when I started. She didn't think I was serious about it. Didn't think I would keep my grades up."

"Oh." The extent of how little she was needed was beginning to hit home.

"If you can't take me, Dad said he could probably pick me up after work most days. Don't worry if you can't."

"No, I can. I still need to check on Eleanor and the twins." Insecurity rippled through her chest. Was she was being replaced? At least Blackburn still needed her skill as a vet. She wondered how long it would be till Seth found someone to replace her.

Henry came out of the farm house with old man Blackburn. Grace had decided that was what she was going to call him now, not Seth's grandfather. It would be a business relationship. Strictly business. The way Abel wanted it.

"How's it going?" Henry asked.

"I'm almost done, Dad. But can I stay longer? Maybe ride Lady? Grace will drive me home, won't you?"

Grace was about to agree when Henry answered. "No riding that horse without your mother's say so. She's the horse person, not me. What would I be able to do if you ran into any problems?"

"There won't be any problems."

"No, there won't because you're coming home with me. Grace is nice enough to drive you home all those times after school. We can't impose on her for more than that." Caroline rolled her eyes and frowned as she left with her father.

"What are you doing about feeding the horses in the morning and making sure they have water?" Grace asked Lamar. "Caroline can't do that."

"No, my grandson has it all taken care of, or so he tells me. The housekeeper is going to put food out for them each morning and let them out into the pasture unless it's too cold. Then when Caroline comes, she'll bring them back in, brush them down, put them back in their stalls and feed them."

"Then I guess you don't need me."

"That's what I told my grandson. I don't need you till it's time for those foals to be born. That's how we used to do it, back in Kentucky."

"And what did your grandson say?"

"Something about twins being a complicated pregnancy and that you needed to check in on them from time to time."

"That I do."

Blackburn walked over to the stall and reached over to run his hand down Lady's nose. This was the first time Grace had seen him have any contact with any of the horses.

"That grandson of mine keeps telling me I'm too old to take care of these horses. I told him I've been taking care of horses since I could walk. I don't need all this extra help."

"Maybe when you're stronger. Or in the spring when the weather's better. He's just concerned about you."

"He's only concerned about his inheritance — his and his brother's. He's afraid I'm going to blow all of my money on these horses." Blackburn continued to rub Lady's nose, then he went into the stall and rubbed the colt. "He's a pretty one, isn't he?"

"Yes, he is. How are you going to train him?"

"I thought you were going to do that. Isn't that what the trip down to Kentucky was all about? You and Seth were going to train him, and the other babies once they are born. That's what Seth told me. That was the plan. I should have known better. Seth never could stick with anything."

"Is that why he had to leave?"

"Had to leave? Is that what Seth told you?"

"Yes."

Old man Blackburn shook his head but didn't offer any explanation. Grace decided it was better not to pursue the matter further.

"Tell me about your farm down in Kentucky. Why did you leave?"

"When you are the fourth of four boys, there really isn't enough farm to go around, like I told you before. My oldest brother Roy, he got the farm. Albert worked it with him. Sam took up blacksmithing. Wasn't much left for me so I decided to take my chances with going north to work in the auto industry. There was good money to be made. The union made sure of that. Not as good now, but back then you had a job for life and good benefits." His voice trailed off.

"Don't you think you should go back in where it's warm?"

"Now don't you go fussing after me too. I'm not a doddering old fool, not yet anyway. Between my grandsons and that housekeeper, and now you, you'd think I can't feed myself, much less find my way from the house to the barn."

"I didn't mean to imply any such thing." The housekeeper called for him. "I think it's time for dinner."

"Wouldn't do well to keep the woman waiting. She does feed me and launder my clothes." He patted Lady one last time. "So, will you still be coming over here every night now that Seth's gone?"

"That's the plan, at least until those foals are safely delivered."

Blackburn grunted then headed to the house without saying goodbye. Maybe Grace had another reason to visit besides the horses.

Chapter 23

Grace was grateful to be back to her work routine after the break for the holidays. Work helped her push problems out of the fore-front of her mind and put them in perspective. Seth had been gone for over two weeks with no word. Had she expected anything different? She had hoped for something else but was adjusting to the reality.

"Your nine o'clock is here." Adah knocked on her office door.

"Okay. I'll be right there." Grace picked up the clipboard that held the patient's chart. Routine heartworm check and exam. Male, neutered, Lab, nine years old.

Grace opened the exam room door. A chocolate Lab waddled to her, tail wagging. His muzzle was flecked with grey hair. His owner, Mrs. Russell, filled the chair to overflowing with her bulk. Her grey hair was pulled up into a bun on her head.

"How much does he weigh?" Grace asked, then looked at the chart for her answer. Over a hundred pounds. "He's a good thirty pounds or more overweight."

"He does like his treats," the Irish woman said in response.

"We've talked about this before, haven't we?"

"Every year."

"And yet every year he continues to gain weight at a rate of five pounds or more a year."

"I try, but it's me husband. He can't resist sharing his snacks with old Kiernan here. Every night he sits down with a bowl of Cheez-Its or popcorn and shares with Kiernan. Two for him, one for Kiernan. I tell him it's no good to be feeding that dog so much. Not good for me husband either, but he still does it. He eats a burger and gives the last bite to the dog. Has a bowl of ice cream, he lets the last spoonful melt till it's runny — the way Kiernan here likes it. It's hard to resist his face. Look at him. How can you say no to such a face?" Mrs. Russell put her hands on either side of the Lab's face and talked to him.

"Yes, he's clearly starving. A regular ad for the ASPCA, except that he's so big he can hardly walk. You know Labs, they'll eat till they puke, and then eat the puke."

"Yes, he has done that once or twice."

"You're going to have to put him on a strict diet." Grace moved her hands over the rolls of flesh, seeking out lumps and abnormalities. The extra pounds made it next to impossible. "No more snacks, no treats. One cup of dog food in the morning, one at night."

"Me husband's the one you need to talk to."

"Tell him, if you don't get Kiernan's weight down, you'll be looking at all kinds of expensive health problems. He's already developing arthritis in his knees. Does your husband want to pay for knee replacements?"

"That he doesn't."

"Then Kiernan needs to lose weight. Maybe they could go on a diet together."

"Right you are. It would be good for both of them."

"You can train your dog, but much harder to train a husband."

"They do tend to do what they want. You married?"

"No." Grace brushed off the question.

"A smart young woman like you? I would think you'd have plenty of suitors."

"We don't call them suitors now, but no, I don't."

"I've a grandson. You'll like him. Should I have him call you?"

"Oh, well, actually, I have been seeing someone. He's out of town right now."

"So, you're unattached. You'll love Robbie. I'll have him give you a call." Mrs. Russell stood up. Rolls of fat pushed out around the belt of her dress as she struggled to walk, holding Kiernan's leash. It seemed it wasn't just her dog that needed a diet.

Grace went back to her office to finish making notes on Kiernan's chart.

"Mrs. Russell trying to fix you up with Robbie again?" Jill asked when she sat down.

"Every year, it's the same thing."

"And every year Kiernan is another five pounds heavier."

"Right. How'd you know?"

"You forget, Kiernan was my patient for years before you started seeing him."

Grace made some notes on his chart then picked up the chart for her next patient.

"Can you take my ten o'clock?" Jill asked.

"What's up?"

"I got a call from a local dairy farmer. Something with one of their cows. Unless you'd rather take the call."

Grace was tempted. She had always thought she wanted to work with small animals, dogs and cats and the occasional gerbil or guinea pig, rather than large animals. Usually vets focus on one or the other. Since working with the horses at Blackburn farm, she was starting to rethink that decision. Maybe she should consider specializing in farm animals. Jill would be happy to turn it over to her. There really weren't enough farm animals around to keep a full-time vet busy, but they still needed someone to do the work.

Emergency calls all hours of the night or day? Driving out into the country? She liked getting out of the four walls of the clinic. Liked driving in the country to see her patients in their natural "habitat," though she didn't like those early morning emergency calls. Maybe it was worth exploring further.

"I'll take the call if you take my ten o'clock."

"Sounds fair to me."

Grace drove her car over the icy dirt driveway, slipping all the way. If she was going to change over to large animals, she would need a car more suited to driving on Michigan's snow-and-ice-covered roads. Maybe a Range Rover, or at least a truck with four-wheel drive, not her little Volkswagen bug. She made it safely to the barn, threw her old galoshes on over her shoes and sludged her way inside where she was greeted by a young man around her age in Carhartt overalls and a heavy corduroy jacket. She had expected an old farmer, more like old man Blackburn, rather than someone young.

"I'm Jeffrey." The young man reached out his hand in introduction. "Where's Dr. Bennet? I was expecting someone older."

"I'm her associate. She couldn't make it." She expected this from the older farmers but not someone so clearly her contemporary. The old farmers didn't trust anyone young enough to be their grandchildren. They wanted the "real" vet. She had to prove herself to them. Age had little to do with pre-judging. It was something everyone did to some extent.

"I was expecting Dr. Bennet."

"And I was expecting someone much older," Grace countered. "So, we're even."

"Sorry. Wasn't thinking. Our milk cows. They're not producing like they were. I looked it up on the internet. I think they have mastitis."

"That would be the most likely diagnosis. Let's take a look." Mastitis was common in cows. A nuisance but easily treated with antibiotics.

The cows were warm and clean in their stalls. A good sign.

"Have they been out in the mud or manure recently?"

"During the thaw last week. We let them out to pasture and they rolled around in the mud."

"That could account for it." Grace reached for the first cow's teats. The udder was clearly full. The first three teats released milk easily when she massaged them. The fourth was backed up. She couldn't get any milk out. The second cow had similar problems, two of the teats didn't work.

"They will need a round of antibiotics. I need to get a sample of milk from the infected teats and take it to the clinic for testing to know what antibiotic to prescribe." Larger vet operations, ones that specialized in farm animals, had trucks complete with testing kits to save the hassle of waiting. They also carried antibiotics to give to the animals, but that wasn't the case with their primarily small animal clinic. She was grateful that she had taken that elective on bovine health while in vet school. There she had learned how to milk a cow and diagnose common problems. This was her first time using that knowledge in the field.

Grace took her sample. "Once I have this tested, I'll call and you can get the prescription. Let me show you how to administer the antibiotics when you get them." Grace grabbed the swollen teat. "You need to clear the teat as much as possible of any milk to make room for the antibiotic. Then you inject the antibiotic and massage backwards to push it up into the udder, hold it to keep it from flowing out. There will be directions with the prescription. Just follow them." Who was she to tell this man what to do? She had only done it once herself, under supervision. She was the blind, leading the blind. Still she made it sound like she knew what she was doing.

They were joined by a young woman with her coat open over a swollen stomach.

"Dr. Reese, this is my wife, Debra."

"Would you like to come in for coffee or hot tea? Something to take the chill off?"

Grace was going to say no, say she was needed at the clinic. She was needed, but she was needed here too. What would ten minutes matter?

"Thank you. Hot coffee would be nice."

"You girls go ahead. I've got work to finish here."

Now that she had dealt with the presenting problem, Grace had the leisure to access her surroundings. It was a nice size barn, with several empty stalls. A quarter horse stood in the farthest stall.

"I see you have a horse," Grace said.

"Yes, that's old Sam. He came with the farm. The owner didn't have any use for him. We didn't have the heart to have him put down, so now he's ours," Debra said.

"Mind if I look at him while I'm here?"

"Of course not. We'd appreciate it. I'll put on the coffee. Come up to the house when you're ready."

Grace walked up to the horse, letting him see her out of both eyes before silently getting permission from him to approach. She rubbed his nose and surveyed the massive body. He stood a full foot over her.

"He must have been impressive in his day," Grace said when Jeffrey approached.

"He was a good plow horse, I've been told. I'm thinking about maybe hooking him up to a plow this spring and seeing how he does. Just enough for a nice garden. We have a small farm. We don't need or want a lot of expensive equipment like the big, commercial farms. We can't compete with those farms anyway."

"How will you make a living?"

"We have a small restaurant in town. We'll be growing food for that."

Farm to table. Grace was familiar with the concept. It was big in Kalamazoo and other cities. Late in coming to Cascade Falls. The concept was to only use locally grown food.

"That, and my wife has a popular podcast. The money she makes helped us purchase this land. Small business loans helped us buy the restaurant. Now we need Mother Nature and a few good years before we are profitable."

"Risky business."

"Maybe so. Especially for a city boy like me, but Debra loves farms and I love Debra."

Grace doubted it was that simple.

"And I'm interested in getting back to nature, away from all the technology, noise and pollution of big cities," Jeffrey added.

"But you're still reliant on technology for Debra's podcast."

"I didn't say we wanted to get away from all technology. Technology is useful as long as you don't let it run your life. I ought to know. I used to do IT for a company in Chicago. Still do some on a consultant basis."

"So you aren't entirely reliant on your farm?"

"Not yet. But we hope to be. You better head up to the house before the coffee gets cold."

Jeffrey pointed out the path to the house. Grace took her time, stepping carefully on snow-covered patches of ice along the way. She saw a hen house. What farm didn't have a hen house? Especially if they wanted the eggs for a restaurant. And if she wasn't mistaken, there was a bee hive. Very ambitious for a couple her age with a baby on the way.

The farm house had seen better days, but the kitchen was warm and sunny and smelled of coffee and fresh baked peanut butter cookies.

"Try one. I'm experimenting with different recipes. I sell them at the small store down the road."

"The one where they sell Amish baked goods?" Grace was only vaguely aware of the store. She had not checked it out herself yet. She had heard the breads and pies were outstanding. But who needed Amish pies when you had your grandma's pies?

"Yes, you should check it out on your way back. Once we get the restaurant up and running, I'll be selling baked goods there."

"That and running your podcast and taking care of a baby," Grace added.

"You've been talking to Jeffrey. The podcast is no big deal. I can run it out of the house."

"That's not what Jefferey says. He says it's a big deal. He's pretty proud of you." Grace took a sip of coffee. Strong. Like she liked it. "When are you due?"

"This spring. Late March or early April. Like the farm animals."

"The farm animals I can help you with. The other …"

Debra laughed. "That's taken care of. I've got a midwife."

Now how did Grace know she would have a midwife? These back-to-nature couples always wanted midwives, suspicious of modern medicines.

"I also have a doctor who works with my midwife in case you were wondering. We aren't opposed to modern medicine or technology. We just would like to have a natural birth, like God intended."

"That's pretty much what your husband told me." Grace took a bite of cookie. "I didn't realize there were any Amish families in the area."

"There's a farm just down the road from us. They keep to themselves."

"Naturally."

"If you do much work with farm animals, you'll get to know them. You can learn a lot from them."

Grace looked around the kitchen. Quaint. They had the avocado green appliances that were the hallmark of some earlier era. "This house a fixer-upper?"

"Yes, that's why we can afford it. The basic foundation and frame are solid. It does need modern plumbing and electrical wiring."

"And Jeffrey is doing that?"

"He is learning, but no. We've got a home improvement team coming out to work on the house. They videotape the repairs and run it on their program. In exchange we get free labor."

"Now how did I know that?" Grace took another bite of cookie. "Delicious."

"Take some back with you for Dr. Bennet and the staff." Debra started to put a dozen into a plastic bag. She added some business cards as Grace tried to protest. "All I ask is that you put my business cards out with them. It's good business. If you want to make it as an entrepreneur you have to use every opportunity to advertise."

Grace thanked Debra for the cookies and waved at Jeffrey on her way out.

It seems everyone has an angle.

The prospect of focusing on farm animals followed her all afternoon and into the evening.

"What has you so serious?" her dad asked as he sat down with her while she ate her warmed-over dinner. It had become a routine since she started staying late at the Blackburn farm.

"Jill suggested I might want to specialize in farm animals. It would be a good addition to the clinic."

"Doesn't Jill already do that?"

"Yes, but just on a limited basis. Any real problems, we refer them to the vet in Hillsdale."

"I didn't think there were enough farms around to keep a vet busy."

"That's what I thought too, but it seems there are more farms than I was aware of. Small farms cropping up, where the owners keep a few animals for their own consumption or a small market while they work other positions. There could be more work than I thought."

"Depends on whether that's what you want to do."

"I know. It's different animals and different people. Pet owners, they treat their pets like their children. Sometimes that's good. Other times it's not so good. No matter how much they may think of an animal as part of the family, they're still animals, not humans, and need to be treated as such."

"Sounds like you've seen a lot."

"You remember the TV show, Green Acres?" Grace had watched the show reruns a few times. "Arnold Ziffle, the pig that attended school. Remember? Mr. Ziffle treated him like his own son, even sent him to school. That's nothing." Grace started laughing.

"You're teasing me now."

"Gotcha, Dad." Usually she was on the receiving end of these jokes. "No, it's not as bad as that, but close."

"Farm animals are working animals," Grace continued. "They need to work for their living. Cows give milk, steers are bred for slaughter, chickens lay eggs. If they don't produce or can't do their jobs, they are gone. Killed and eaten. I don't know how I'd feel about that."

"And horses? How do they fit in?"

"Horses used to provide transportation. They worked, hauling buggies, pulling plows. But now, they no longer have their jobs to do."

"Does that make them obsolete? Ready to be put out to pasture?"

"No." Grace paused as she searched for the right words. What was it about horses? They were expensive to purchase and maintain. They didn't earn their keep. They weren't valuable as food, at least not in this country. And they were a lot of work. It seemed there was no reason to keep horses. So why keep them then? "They are gifts of God's free grace. They are beauty and spirit."

"That they are, daughter. And so are you." Her dad stood up and squeezed her shoulders. "I hope you don't have to go out in the country tomorrow. They're predicting an ice storm."

"Thanks for the warning, Dad." Grace checked the weather app on her phone. Yes, there was the possibility of an ice storm, but the app was wrong half as much as it was right. Still, a day off of work because of the ice storm shutting everything down … Sweet.

Chapter 24

Grace shut off the alarm then checked the local news. As predicted, an ice storm had rolled through overnight. Schools were closed. That meant the clinic would be closed. She rolled over to get some extra sleep. No luck. Something was bothering her, but what? Why couldn't she have a day off like everyone else? Why couldn't she just turn her brain off and go back to sleep?

She had almost drifted back to sleep when she woke with a start. Blackburn farm. Who was feeding the horses if Mr. Blackburn's housekeeper couldn't make it there because of the storm? Had Abel made alternate arrangements in the event of an emergency?

Grace rolled over in bed and checked her phone. Eight-thirty. Was it too early to call? She knew Mrs. Hill usually arrived around eight. She should be there to answer the phone. Grace rang the number. No answer. She got up and got dressed then called again. Again, no answer. She went down for breakfast.

"What are you doing up?" her dad asked. "I figured you'd sleep till noon."

Ava got up and poured her a cup of coffee. "Since you're up, are you ready for breakfast? I'm making French toast."

"I don't know." Grace called Blackburn farm again. Still no answer.

"What's wrong?" her dad asked.

"I've been calling Blackburn farm. There's no answer."

"Doesn't he have a housekeeper? I'm sure everything's okay," Ava said.

"But what if she couldn't make it because of the ice storm?"

"I'm sure the horses will be fine. They're in a protected structure. They won't die if they miss one meal," her dad said.

"It's not the horses I'm worried about. What if Mr. Blackburn tries to go to the barn to feed them?"

"He wouldn't do that, would he? Wouldn't he know better?" Ava asked.

"Would he? He's pretty stubborn." Grace could see him trying to trudge across the icy path to the barn, slipping, falling, unable to get up, lying there for hours before anyone found him. "I've got to go."

"Not in your car. Not alone. We'll use my car. Nothing is good on ice, but my Buick is heavier and has all-wheel drive. Just give me a minute to get ready."

Grace sat at the table and drank her coffee.

"At least eat something," Ava said. "Cereal. Toast. Bread with peanut butter?"

"Nothing sounds good."

Her dad came back downstairs in jeans and a heavy flannel shirt. Grace followed him to the garage. He threw his winter coat on then put heavy bags in the trunk of his car.

"What are you doing?" Grace asked.

"Sand bags. In case we need them. They'll also add weight." Then he added some bags of water softener pellets. "More weight."

"Be careful." Ava waved as she watched them pull out of the garage and onto the ice-covered driveway.

Her dad crawled down the street. Every time it seemed the road was clear and they picked up speed, they slid on a patch of ice and fishtailed. They passed a number of cars in the ditch with their flashers on.

"Can't stop to help," her dad muttered. Grace knew it wasn't like him to drive by anyone in trouble, but this was different. They couldn't stop to help everyone. They would never make it. Who knew what they would find? Electrical lines were down all over the city. Maybe there was no power at the farm. Maybe the phone was out. Maybe that was why he didn't answer. They'll find him safe in the house. They would insist on him coming back with them. That was her best-case scenario. She didn't want to think about the worse.

It took over an hour to get to the farm. Even as they pulled down the driveway, Grace feared ending in a ditch. At least now they were here. She smelled death. She prayed she was wrong.

Grace stepped carefully on the ice on her way to the house. The power was on but no one answered her call. Mrs. Hill's car was nowhere to be seen. That left only one place.

She met her dad outside the house. "Not here."

"Then let's go to the barn. Hopefully he's there."

They didn't go far before finding him lying on the path.

"Mr. Blackburn, are you all right?" Grace squatted down next to him. No response. She took his pulse. "He has a pulse, just weak. It looks like he may have hit his head."

"We've got to get him out of here." Her dad slipped his arm under Blackburn's arm and lifted. Grace took the other side. Together they walked him back to the farmhouse, up the steps and into the warm kitchen.

"I wonder how long he's been out there. We've got to get him to a hospital." Grace continued to check his pulse and look for signs of life.

"Ambulances find it hard in this weather too. Better to take him ourselves than wait for the ambulance."

Blackburn moaned and moved his head.

"It looks like he's coming out of it. Mr. Blackburn, can you hear me?" Grace's dad shouted in his ear.

"Of course I can. I'm not deaf." The old man shook his head. "Where am I? What happened? The last I remember I was going to feed the horses."

"We found you on the path, unconscious," Grace explained.

"That's right. I slipped and fell, bumping my head. That's all I remember." He reached up to a spot on his head where blood was caked.

"The cold must have frozen the blood," Grace said. "How are you? Do you have feeling everywhere?"

"Unfortunately I feel every ache and pain in my body."

Grace smiled. "That's good. I'm checking for frostbite. It sounds like you're okay. We should still get you to the hospital to get checked out."

"No one's putting me back in that hospital."

"Just to make sure nothing's broken." Grace looked for signs of frost bite. Lamar had been well insulated. He had on thermal boots and gloves and a warm coat. The only place exposed was his face. Grace checked a suspicious spot. It was cool to touch but seemed to be warming nicely.

"If you'll excuse me, I'd like to change my clothes. Seems I had an accident when I fell." Lamar stood up then fell back down into his chair. "Woozy. Give me another minute."

He tried to stand up again, then passed out in the chair.

"He may have a concussion. We have to get him to the hospital." Grace checked his pulse again. Faint.

"I'll get a change of clothes for him. What about the horses?"

"I'll make sure they are okay and have enough food for the day. Then we can go." Grace looked to see his chest move. "At least he's breathing."

Grace walked to the barn, carefully moving on the ice. She filled the horses' feed bags, enough to last till tomorrow if she couldn't get back, broke the ice cover over their water trough so they could drink, then gave them a quick rub before leaving. That would have to do.

Her dad was already helping Mr. Blackburn to the car when she came back.

"He regained consciousness so he was able to walk some," her dad said as he eased him into the back seat. He put the car in gear, proceeded up the driveway then drove to the hospital. Grace called ahead to alert them to the situation.

"Got it. Eighty-year-old man, fall on ice, possible concussion," the clerk repeated after Grace. "We'll be ready for you. Estimated time of arrival?"

"When do you think we'll get there, Dad? They want an ETA."

"Tell them we'll get there when we get there."

Chapter 25

They waited in the emergency room with old man Blackburn. Seems he had suffered a concussion, but a mild one.

"You're lucky. It could have been much worse if this young lady and her father hadn't come along," the ER doctor told them.

"If that's the case, let me out of here," Lamar said.

"Not so fast. We need to keep you overnight for observation. Just to be on the safe side. And then we need to discuss discharge." He turned and faced Grace and her father. "Are you next of kin?"

"No, just friends of the family."

"The hospital case worker will be in to discuss whether it's safe for him to be living alone."

"What are you talking about? You kicking me out of my home?"

"Just hospital protocol in such cases. We have to discuss options."

"There are no options. There is only one option. I'm going to my home."

"What do we do in the meantime?" Grace's dad asked.

"We'll be getting him a room upstairs as soon as one's ready. We're short-handed because of the ice storm. A number of employees couldn't make it in. But it shouldn't take long."

Grace and her father were given Lamar's room number when hospital staff came to move him.

"You can meet him upstairs," the orderly told them as they rolled him out.

"Do you want to get something to eat?" her dad asked.

"No. Besides, I don't know that the cafeteria is open." Grace pulled out her phone. "I better call Seth and Abel. They'll want to know."

"And I better call Ava." Both stepped aside to make their calls.

Grace was put through to Seth's voice mail. "This is Seth. You know what to do." She had been hoping to talk to him, hadn't spoken to him since Christmas Eve. Guess it wasn't going to happen, at least not now.

"Seth, it's Grace. Your grandfather fell on the ice and hit his head. He's in the hospital with a mild concussion. Nothing serious. Just keeping him for observation. I thought you would want to know." Grace hesitated. How should she sign off? Love? Miss you? "Bye." She clicked off, took a breath and called Abel.

"Yes," a gruff voice answered.

"Abel, this is Grace Reese, the vet."

"Yes," the voice softened. "Grace. Is everything all right?"

"That's why I'm calling. Your grandfather slipped on the ice and fell."

"Is he okay?"

"The doctors think he has a mild concussion. Nothing serious but they're keeping him in the hospital for observation."

"He's in the hospital? Can I talk to him?"

"They're taking him upstairs to his room right now. Once he's settled, you'll be able to call his room."

"Should I drive there?"

Grace looked over at her dad. He had finished his call and was standing next to her. "He wants to know whether he should come here. What should I tell him?"

"Here, let me talk to him." Grace put the phone on speaker and handed it to her dad. "Mr. Blackburn?"

"Barton, Abel Barton."

"Abel, this is Grace's father, Dale. There's no need for you to drive here today. He's doing fine and is safe in the hospital. The roads are bad throughout lower Michigan. It's not safe to drive today. Tomorrow will be soon enough as long as the roads are clear. He may need you to be here before they will discharge him."

"I'll be there."

"No rush. Be safe."

"Thank you," Abel said as he signed off.

"Were you able to get hold of Seth?"

"No, but I left a message."

"Ava said she'd have dinner ready whenever we get home. Now let's see how our patient is doing."

Grace figured she already knew how Mr. Blackburn was doing. Just as ornery as ever and ready to get out.

She was right.

Chapter 26

The roads were clear by the next morning. This was Michigan after all. Michiganders are used to snow and ice. They know how to handle them. It takes more than a sheet of ice to keep the state closed. The main roads were clear and passable. She went into the clinic but was able to leave early because of cancellations due to the ice storm. The gravel road to the farm was not entirely clear of ice, and the driveway remained treacherous. Grace wished she had driven her dad's car.

She breathed a sigh of relief when her car finally came to a stop, short of hitting the barn as it slid on a patch of ice. She wondered if the horses had been fed yet. She saw Abel's black BMW. Old man Blackburn was no longer her concern.

The horses were still in their stalls. Grace led them out of the barn and into the corral to give them a little exercise after being cooped up for two days. Then she went back into the barn to check on food and water. Caroline had called to let her know she couldn't come over. School was closed and she didn't have a way to get there. Grace assured her that she would take care of the horses.

"It seems I owe you another thank you for saving my grandfather's life." The deep voice rumbled through the empty barn, catching her off guard.

"It was what anybody would have done."

"I assure you not everybody would have come out in an ice storm to check on an old man, an ornery one at that. If you hadn't come over … I hate to think what would have happened, how long my grandfather would have lain on that ground before being found."

Was that a crack in his burly exterior? She almost thought she heard a catch in his voice as he spoke. Couldn't be. "My dad helped."

"I'm trying to thank you. Why are you being so difficult?"

"You're welcome." Grace continued to pour feed for the horses, her back to Abel. "Are you satisfied now?"

"No, I'm not. I usually like to look into the eyes of the person I'm thanking."

"Very well." Grace turned and faced him; her face tight with anger.

"What's wrong? Why are you so angry? What did I do to you?"

"Look, I accepted your thank you. Now, if you'll excuse me, I have work to do."

Abel took hold of her arm to prevent her from returning to her chores. "I can't excuse you. Not just yet. I have to talk to you."

"So talk." Grace shook his hand loose from her arm and crossed her arms in front of her.

"Not like this. It would be better if maybe you could meet me up at the house, so we can sit down and talk."

"Look, if you want to talk, talk. Otherwise, I have work to do."

"Okay," Abel sighed. "Have it your way. This incident proved to me what I've been worried about all along. It's just not safe for my grandfather, living here all alone. So, I was wondering …" Abel took a deep breath before continuing. "Would you consider moving in for a while to make sure my grandfather is safe?"

Grace's mouth dropped open. Was he kidding?

"Before you say anything, hear me out. You're already over here every day as it is. Wouldn't it be easier to stay? You yourself said that the closer Eleanor gets to having her babies, the more closely she'll need to be watched. What better place to watch her than here? You don't have to do anything. The housekeeper will prepare meals for you. All you have to do is be here at night so my grandfather isn't alone. I'll pay for your time."

"What about getting someone from a home health agency?"

"My grandfather won't have anything to do with them. I already asked. He refuses to have a stranger in his home. And it's not like he needs assistance with day-to-day living, getting dressed or everyday activities. Believe me, I wouldn't be asking if I had other options."

Grace believed him. "Maybe you should have thought about this before you kicked Seth out."

"What are you talking about?"

"You heard me. Before you kicked Seth out. He said you were forcing him to move out."

"That's what he said?"

"Yes."

"And you believed him?" Abel's face clouded over. He was hiding something, but what?

"I didn't have any reason not to."

"Seth left of his own free will, because he wasn't willing to clean up his messes."

"What does that mean?"

"It can mean whatever you want it to mean. You'll believe what you want. Clearly this is a mistake. I'll work something out." Abel started for the barn door.

He would work something out? What did that mean? What if he put old man Blackburn in a retirement home? That would surely kill him. And what about the horses? If Blackburn no longer lived here, what was there to keep Abel from selling them?

"Mr. Barton … Abel, wait," Grace called after him. She caught up with him halfway back to the house. "I've thought about your offer, and if it's still on the table, yes. But on my terms. I'll not accept any money for staying with your grandfather. You're right. This will make it easier for me to keep an eye on Eleanor. I won't be beholden to you. I'll only accept the pay rightfully mine for veterinary services rendered. Deal?" Grace extended her hand.

He turned towards her, his face dark and unreadable. "Are you sure you want to deal with someone so clearly despicable in your mind?"

"It's not exactly my first choice, but if it means your grandfather stays in his own home and keeps the farm …"

"You think I would ship my grandfather off to a nursing home? That would kill him." His eyes blazed with anger and …? Hurt? Offence? Sadness? Had she misjudged him?

"I'm sorry if I misjudged you. I hardly know you."

"You're right — you don't. And I hardly know you." Abel started back on his way to the farmhouse.

"Abel, wait. I said I'm sorry. I do want to help out. I've grown fond of your grandfather and the horses. Deal?"

Abel stopped and faced her. "It's not like I have any better alternatives. I guess we both have little choice but to trust each other. Deal." He squeezed her hand in a tight grasp. "Once again you have saved me." She saw the relief in his eyes despite his recent anger.

"I haven't saved you."

"By saving my grandfather, you have saved me."

Grace shrugged. This was a side of Abel she hadn't been aware of. "When do you want me to start?"

"I'll be staying through the weekend, so Sunday will be soon enough. First I have to break the news to my grandfather."

"That should prove interesting." She smiled as she imagined Lamar's response to the proposal.

"You want to do it?" He returned her smile.

"Oh, no. I'll leave that in your capable hands."

"Okay." Abel extended his hand, again enveloping hers in a firm handshake. "I guess I'll be seeing you around then."

"I guess you will." Grace watched as he ambled to the house. What had she done?

Chapter 27

Her dad had been understanding of her decision. He recognized the logic involved.

"This way I don't have to worry about you driving out there in another ice storm or a snow storm. This is Michigan after all. And it's not forever."

"We'll still see you now and then, won't we? You're not going to disappear from our lives the way Ashley and Jacob did when they moved out, are you?" Ava asked.

"I'll be at every Sunday dinner. You can count on that. I'm not moving away from Cascade Falls."

The harder sell had been old man Blackburn. Abel was still there Sunday afternoon when she arrived after Sunday dinner.

"I thought I should stick around and help you move in." Abel took her suitcase from her.

"Not a lot to move. Just my clothes and some books. If I need anything else, it's not far to drive home and get it."

"That's not exactly what I meant." Abel nodded in the direction of the living room where his grandfather was watching TV.

"Don't worry about him. I'm good with old people. He won't stay angry forever."

"You underestimate my grandfather's ability to hold a grudge."

"And how long is that?"

"He's still holding a grudge against my mother for something that happened over thirty years ago."

"That is a long time. Is that why your mother never visits?"

"The only person who can hold a grudge longer than my grandfather is my mother, but that's a story for another time. Let's get you settled."

Abel carried the suitcase up the stairs and showed her to her room. It was square with a sloping wall on one side, cutting into the space but making the room so much more interesting. Like Josie's home. Grace remembered the secret passageways in Josie's home that had provided shelter for runaway slaves. Maybe there would be similar passageways here.

The double bed was neatly made with a set of towels awaiting her use. There was a closet, a chest of drawers and a small desk with chair. A space heater sat next to the desk, working overtime to chase the chill away.

"Old houses. You know how drafty they can be. I hope it's all right. Grandpa's room is on the first floor. I had an office converted to a bedroom so he wouldn't have to climb stairs. There's a bathroom across the hall. It's all yours. Though you may want to use the one downstairs for showers. It takes forever for the water to get hot, and when it does, it runs out quickly."

"I'll manage," Grace assured him.

"I'm sorry it isn't nicer." Abel scanned the room again, as if looking for a good point he had missed.

"No, it's fine. I like old houses. So much more interesting than the new ones they are building."

"I'm going to try to make it over here on weekends as often as possible. If you want to go home then, you can. My room's down the hall from yours. There's also an extra bedroom you can use if you need more space."

"I'm sure I'll be fine."

"Well then, I guess I'll be leaving. There's food in the refrigerator. Help yourself. Mrs. Hill fixes a big Sunday dinner in the afternoon then leaves something light for later. That way she can leave early and have more time at home."

"Thank you. I'll find it if I'm hungry."

"Thank you again. You don't know how much this means to me." He locked onto her eyes as he sought words. Grace shifted her gaze away from the deep, probing eyes and bit her lip.

"Oh, I think I have an idea. You better go. Traffic will be impossible around Chicago."

"Remember, you have my phone number. Use it." The corner of his lip curled up in a slight smile. "Good luck with my grandfather."

"Get out of here so I can unpack." Grace pushed him out the door. She wondered about his reluctance to leave. Maybe he wasn't the cold, hard business man she thought him to be.

Grace hung up her clothes in the closet and filled the dresser drawers. When everything was put away, she decided to visit the horses, bring them in for the night and feed them. She had talked to Caroline and told her she would be staying there and could take care of feeding the horses any time Caroline couldn't make it.

"Thanks, Grace." Grace heard the relief in Caroline's voice. "It was harder to do every day than I thought it would be. I was missing out on every after-school activity. If we could go back to just a few days a week, that would be great."

"That's fine. Will your dad be able to pick you up?"

"As long as it's not every day, he'll be okay with it."

Grace didn't mind the extra work. She was happy for the excuse to spend more time around the horses.

"I'm going to the barn to feed the horses, Mr. Blackburn. Do you need anything before I go?"

"I'm perfectly capable of getting anything I need. You aren't here as my nurse maid."

"I wasn't offering as a nurse maid, just a courtesy I extend to anyone I share space with."

Blackburn grunted. "And if you're going to be staying here, you might as well call me by my first name, Lamar. None of this 'Mr. Blackburn' any more. Makes me feel old. I may be old. That doesn't mean I have to feel old too."

"Would you rather I call you old man Blackburn?"

"Is that what you call me behind my back?"

"That and other things."

"Fair enough. Call me what you will. Old man Blackburn, Lamar, or whatever, just so you don't call me Mr. Blackburn."

That went well, Grace thought as she went down the back-porch steps and headed to the barn. What was Abel worried about?

Chapter 28

Grace raced up the stairs after her day at the clinic, changed her clothes and headed to the barn. One of the perks of living here. No need to wait till later to get out of her work clothes. No need to worry about getting home late. She could spend as much time with her horses as she wanted once she got home from work.

On her first day in her new home, Lamar had gruffly mumbled something as she came through the door about dinner being in the refrigerator if she wanted to eat.

"Thanks, but I think I'll take care of the horses first while there's still daylight."

"Suit yourself." He walked into the living room where she could hear the TV being turned on.

By the third day, he was joining her as she ate, much like her dad did. By the second week he was waiting for her to get home from work to have dinner with her.

"Dinner is hot and on the table. Those horses can wait while you eat," he insisted. He cleared the table after dinner and put the dishes in the dishwasher while she took care of the horses.

True to his word, Abel showed up each weekend, leaving her free to spend the time at home and staying until she came back on Sunday afternoon.

"You don't have to stay here until she gets back. I'm capable of a few hours alone," Lamar was saying when Grace arrived.

"But what if I like spending time with you, you old goat?"

"It would be the first time. That never was enough to get you to visit before."

"That was then, now is now. And now, it's time for me to leave," he said as he walked past Grace, giving her a hint of a smile as he left.

Seth finally returned her call, reaching her while she was at work. She excused herself from an appointment in order to take the call, going into her office and shutting the door. The call kept breaking up, making it hard to hear. He was calling from somewhere overseas.

"Where are you?"

"On a steamship … sea."

"Where? I couldn't hear you."

"How's Gramps?"

"He's okay, out of the hospital."

"What did you say?"

"He's out of the hospital."

"I'm sorry. You're breaking up."

"Call me …" the call was disconnected. There was no calling back. That had been unsatisfactory, but at least he had called. Now she understood why he hadn't called before. He must be some place with poor phone and internet connection.

"Have you heard from my grandson?" Lamar asked over dinner.

"Actually, he called today, or tried to. It was a bad connection."

"Hmmmph," Lamar muttered and attacked the chicken on his plate. "Chicken again. Is that all that woman knows how to cook?"

"Chicken is good for you. Better than all that red meat."

"I don't see where a steak now and then would hurt."

Grace ate her dinner without responding. They had developed an easy routine. Sometimes they ate in silence, other times Lamar shared stories about his life. After dinner, Lamar would crack open a beer and watch TV while she tended to the horses. Abel had made sure he had channels that showed the old TV shows he liked: war movies, Westerns, crime dramas like *The Untouchables* and *Perry Mason*.

"None of that Netflix stuff you kids like to watch. That was all Seth watched, shows like *The Office*, or those Mutant shows."

At first Grace had retired to her room to read once done with her chores. That got old fast. She realized how much she had come to rely on the presence of other people around her as she wandered the deserted upstairs. She checked out the extra bedroom Abel had mentioned but didn't dare to venture into his room. She wondered if the extra room had been Seth's at one time. If so, there was no sign of his presence, just a room with a bed, a chest of drawers, and a rocking chair. Perhaps her room had been Seth's. Grace tried the rocking chair. Fit perfectly. This was a woman's rocking chair, not big enough for a man, not any of the three men she knew that inhabited the house. Maybe it belonged to Abel and Seth's mother. Or their grandmother.

"Whose rocking chair is it? The one in the spare bedroom?" She asked the next day over dinner.

"Rocking chair?"

"Yes, there's a rocking chair in the spare bedroom. Was it your wife's?"

"Haven't been up there for so long, I forget. That must be Annie's chair, the one she rocked our Maggie in." Lamar leaned back as he relived the memory. "I met her at the UAW Union hall, shortly after I moved to Detroit and started working in the factory. She was the prettiest thing you had ever seen, at least to me, with that curly dark brown hair and bright red lips. Others thought so too. They were always hanging around her.

"So how did you finally meet up?"

"I knew I had to do something pretty spectacular to get her attention. I grabbed the union flag, climbed up into the rafters. I was pretty nimble back then. Skinny too. Some claimed I would have made a great jockey, if I hadn't been so tall."

"Lamar, the Union Hall? Your wife?"

"Oh, yeah, I waved that flag till I had everyone's attention. People were yelling at me to get down. I yelled, 'Anna Schmidt, will you marry me?'"

"And what did she say?"

"What do you think she said? What would any good woman with any lick of sense say under the same circumstances? She said no. So then I said, 'will you go out with me?' Again she said no. I said, 'I'm not coming down until you agree to dance with me.'"

"And she said yes."

"She sure did. And we've been dancing ever since. Until the night she died." He stared past her, the twinkle suddenly gone from his eyes.

"What happened?"

"Drunk driver. I don't like to think about it. It was my fault, you see." He continued to stare at a memory only he could see.

"Were you the driver?"

"No, but I should have been. I should have been the one driving that night. It should have been me hit broadside, and her who lived. She was too good. Why does God always take the good ones?" He shook his head and closed his eyes against the memory.

Grace was relieved when she realized Lamar didn't expect an answer. She didn't know what she could say. God had taken her mother so many years ago. Her mom was a good one too.

"She was going to another one of her church functions, a catechism class or special service or something. I forget what. She wanted me to come with her but I refused." He opened his eyes and looked at her. "Haven't stepped into that church since then."

"But Seth said you attended the Episcopal Church?"

"I do — the times I go. That was the Lutheran church. Annie was Lutheran. Good German Lutheran. She was always wanting me to join up, tried to get me to convert. I told her I was raised Episcopal and I would go to my grave Episcopal. Now I don't go at all, except for Christmas and Easter. If I go then."

"I'm sorry for bringing up such painful memories."

"They are precious memories, memories of my Annie. But enough of this." Lamar stood up from the table and started to clear the dishes.

"Let me help with that," Grace insisted.

"One sad memory and you want to treat me like an invalid. Women," Lamar stated, but he didn't send her away. They worked quietly together, neither speaking, till Grace broke the silence.

"Would you mind if I moved it, the rocking chair, into my room?"

"Don't know why not. It's not doing anyone any good where it is. Annie would be happy that someone was using it."

The dishes stacked in the dishwasher, Lamar proceeded to the living room and Grace to the corral.

Later she dragged the rocking chair into her bedroom. Annie's. She must have rocked her baby in it. Maybe rocked Abel and Seth too, when they were babies. Maybe she rocked in it and read books and dreamed dreams, just like Grace had dreamed dreams over the years. Grace wrapped an afghan around her and curled up in the chair and read.

After several nights alone in the chilly upstairs, she decided to take her book and cell phone downstairs to the much warmer living room. She slipped into an overstuffed chair on the far side of the room from the TV and turned on a light. "You don't mind, do you?" she asked when Lamar gave her a sharp look.

"Suit yourself."

She curled up with a book about horses, tucking her stocking covered feet on the chair under her and ignoring the sound of the TV, randomly checking social media in between chapters. It was harder to ignore Lamar's laughter, especially since he laughed so rarely.

"What's so funny?" Grace looked over at the black and white screen.

"Festus. He always comes up with the darnedest ideas."

"Who's Festus?"

"You don't know Festus? Haven't you ever watched *Gunsmoke*?"

"No."

"Then what did you watch when you were a kid? Oh, I forget. You still are a kid."

"Whatever was on Nickelodeon or the Disney channel, when we watched TV. My parents didn't approve of watching too much TV. My stepmother is a teacher. We only got to watch one hour of TV each night."

"Then what did you do the rest of the time?"

"Homework — plus, we read, made things, played with friends, played games. My brother Jacob loved video games, me, not so much. Chores. There was always something to do."

"When I was a kid, we didn't have a TV."

"What did you do?"

"Went to the movie theater when we could. Most of the time we worked. When you grow up on a farm, there's always chores to be done." Lamar went back to his show, Grace to her book. During a commercial he got up, went into the kitchen and came back with another beer.

Grace looked up when she heard the pop of the bottle top being removed.

"You want a beer?" Lamar asked.

"No, no thank you. I don't drink. I don't like the taste of it."

"That's good. My Annie didn't drink either. I don't approve of women drinking. My Maggie though, that was another story."

"Tell me about her."

"Are you going to keep yapping the whole time you're down here, or are you going to let me watch my shows in peace?"

That shut Grace up. Over the next few weeks she became familiar with all of his favorite shows. *Gunsmoke*, *The Rifleman*, *Bonanza*, *Big Valley*, *Andy Griffith*, *Perry Mason*, but especially Western movies. She got to where she knew some of the actors. John Wayne, of course, Audie Murphy, Jimmy Stewart. She remembered Jimmy Stewart from that Christmas movie her grandma always watched. What was it? Miracle on some street? No, *It's a Wonderful Life*. She remembered watching it with her grandmother every December. That and *White Christmas*.

"You ever watch *The Virginian*?" Lamar asked one night.

"No. What's it about?"

"You'll like it. Good clean Western. Not like the shows they make now with people being blown up and heroes who aren't real heroes, those anti-heroes, who aren't any better than the bad guys when it comes to killing. These men are real men. Men of integrity and honor who respect women."

Grace checked her phone. Nine o'clock. She was ready for a break. She put her book down. What would it hurt to watch a little TV?

"Why do they always refer to him as the Virginian? Doesn't he have a name?"

"No, or if he does, they never use it on the show. It's part of the mystique."

"And it's not even set in Virginia."

"Are you going to watch the show or jibber-jabber? I'm sorry I asked you."

Grace shut up and watched. It wasn't a great drama, or as fast-paced as other shows she watched, but once she got to know the characters, she enjoyed it. She got what Lamar meant about good, clean characters. The cowboys weren't dirty and crude, even after a day of riding the range. They cleaned up mighty nicely too for church socials and dances. After a while, it became part of the evening routine. She would read until nine while Lamar watched what he wanted. Then they would watch *The Virginian* together before going to bed. Sometimes she would make popcorn for them to share as Grace moved over to the couch to see the TV better. It passed the time.

Chapter 29

Grace looked at her phone. Abel. Abel never called her. He was like his brother that way. "I've got to take this." She excused herself and went into her office.

"Abel, what's up?"

"I'm sorry, but something's come up here at work. I can't get away this weekend. Is there any chance you could stay with Grandpa?"

What did she have to keep her from saying yes? It's not like she had any social life. Abel had taken care of that when he ran off Seth. Josie was in California. The only commitment she had each weekend was for Sunday dinner with her family. She didn't want to answer too quickly. Let Abel think she was going over her busy calendar.

"Sure. I guess."

"Great. And you know, you don't have to stay there all day. Just so he's not alone at night."

"I'll work it out."

"Thanks, I owe you."

You bet he did. But she owed him as well. She didn't mind spending time with his grandfather. He wasn't demanding at all. Not like some old people are. He pretty much kept to himself. And she liked his stories, when he shared them. Maybe they'd do a Western movie marathon. She usually spent Saturday there anyway if she didn't have to work. It was her best opportunity to work with the mares. During the week she hardly had time to bring them in, brush them and feed them. If Caroline was there, they were often in for the night by the time Grace got home. She was working on weaning Peanut from Lady. She read it should be done sometime between four and six months. She wanted him weaned before the twins were born.

She also wanted to be able to take Lady to the clinic in April. She couldn't do that with Peanut tagging along. She was checking out the horse trailer she found in the barn, seeing if it needed any repairs. And then, she would have to drive the truck to haul it. She would have to make sure the truck still worked. As far as she knew, it hadn't been driven in a while. Lamar was right. There are always chores to do when you live on a farm, even one that wasn't a working farm.

Lamar was surprised when she sat down to dinner with him.

"I've got bad news. You're stuck with me for the weekend."

"What happened to Abel?"

"Something came up at work."

Lamar grunted. "You know you don't have to be around all weekend. I've got things to do."

"I won't. I have things to do too. But for tonight, we have a date with John Wayne."

"Suit yourself." Lamar lowered his head to slurp his soup, hiding the slight grin on his face.

Grace called her dad to let him know she wouldn't be around that weekend. Her dad put his phone on speaker so Ava could hear as well.

"What about Sunday dinner? You can make it to Sunday dinner, can't you?" Ava asked.

"I don't know. I hate to leave Lamar here alone on Sunday."

"Bring him along. There's always plenty. We'll just add another plate."

"I'll have to check with him."

"He'll love it. He can hang out with your grandma and Peter. It'll be good for him to get out of that house."

"Like I said, I'll check on it."

She brought in two bowls of popcorn for their movie marathon, handed one to Lamar than sat on the couch. "My parents want to know if you would like to come to Sunday dinner."

"Mrs. Hill always makes a nice Sunday dinner for me, but there's no reason why you can't go."

"I know that. You don't have to go. There'll be a lot of people."

"Will there be pie?"

"My grandmother always makes pie."

"And roast beef and gravy?"

"I don't know what's on the menu, but we might have pot roast. It's my grandma's favorite."

"Your grandma sounds like my kind of woman. Is she married?"

"Yes, she is."

"Can't have everything." He shrugged.

"You'll like Peter. But if you don't want to go …"

"Who said anything about not wanting to go? If for no other reason than to keep you from skipping dinner with your family because of me. I'll give Mrs. Hill the day off."

"Okay. I'll pick you up after church."

"I'll be ready. You did say there would be pie?"

"Are you going to jibber-jabber all night or watch the movie?"

Grace got up Sunday morning and went to church. She had considered using being at the farm as an excuse to skip, then realized she wanted to go. She would see her family at dinner, but not her church family. She would miss them if she skipped.

Lamar was ready as promised when she got back from church. He was more than ready. He was dressed in his best "Sunday going to meeting" clothes, as they said on those Westerns.

"You know, this is just my family. You don't have to dress up for them."

"Are they coming straight from church?"

"Yes."

"Then they'll be dressed in their church clothes."

"Some of them, but others will have changed. And young people don't dress up for church like they used to."

"I won't embarrass you by not dressing properly."

"You won't embarrass me, Lamar, no matter what you wear. Just be yourself, your own ornery self."

"That I can do."

Lamar was warmly welcomed by her family, as she knew he would be. Grandma made her famous pot roast with browned potatoes and gravy and carrots. And for dessert, apple pie. Lamar chatted in the living room with Peter while dinner was put on the table.

"So you're the young man that's been keeping our Grace so busy," Aunt Kathleen said over dinner.

"I think you are referring to my grandson," Lamar responded.

"No, you. I've been hearing about all those westerns you've got my niece watching, and all your stories."

"Your niece is a special girl."

"You don't have to tell us that." Grandma smiled over at Grace. Grace shook her head. Family.

Afterwards Lamar shared a beer with Peter and her dad. When it was time to leave, everyone invited him back.

"You're coming back next Sunday — right, Lamar?" Grandma asked.

"That depends. You making your pot roast?"

"I'm afraid it's Kathleen's turn to cook next week." Grandma nodded in Aunt Kathleen's direction.

"Hey, I'm not that bad, besides, Joe will help me," Aunt Kathleen said.

"How about I bring dinner," Lamar suggested.

"Do you have a specialty?" Stephanie asked.

"Just my famous chili. You haven't lived till you've tried my chili."

"Chili sounds good to me," Peter said.

"Then it's decided. I'll bring a big pot of chili next week."

"Lamar, are you forgetting? Abel will be here next weekend," Grace interjected.

"Bring him along. We always have room for more," Peter said.

"You heard him," Lamar told her. "Abel can join us if he wants."

Lamar was happy about the invite. Grace was glad for him but she wasn't sure how happy Abel would be. Or how happy she was.

Chapter 30

Grace heard Lamar's grunt of displeasure all the way up the stairs and into her room where she was changing out of her work clothes that Friday.

"You here," Lamar growled as she came down the stairs.

"What were you expecting? That I would stay away?" Abel looked up at her as she neared the bottom. "I think my grandfather likes having you around more than he likes having me around."

"She's a damn sight better to look at than you."

"I'll give you that much." Abel smiled at Grace. "I came early. Thought I would take you out for dinner, both of you, to make up for last weekend. That is if you are free. I gave Mrs. Hill the night off."

"There's no need to do that," Grace insisted.

"I know. I want to do this."

"I have other plans."

"Then tomorrow night."

"I don't know."

"Do you have plans?"

Grace hesitated. Lying didn't come easily to her. "No."

"Then you do now. And for tonight, I guess it's just you and me," he told his grandfather. "Where do you want to go, old man?"

"Any place as long as I don't have to eat chicken. Oh, and I need to stop at the grocery store. I'm making chili for Sunday dinner."

"You are?" Abel looked over at Grace.

"Yes, I am, for Grace's family."

"My family invited your grandfather to Sunday dinner last week. He enjoyed it so much he promised to make chili this week," Grace explained.

"No wonder he wasn't happy to see me. A big family meal on Sunday."

"You're invited too," Lamar said.

Abel looked at Grace before responding. "I'll see."

Grace didn't know why Abel angered her so. He just did. Even when he was trying to be nice, she ended up angry at him. He thinks she's so pathetic that she has nothing better to do than sit around with an old man every night watching Westerns on TV. That's why he wanted to take her out. It was a pity date. The problem was, she was that pathetic. She had no social life. What social life she had, had left with Seth. She had friends from church but most of them were married and raising kids. They weren't interested in going out with her. And if they did, all they talked about was their kids. She had friends from vet school, but they had gone their separate way after graduation. Where would she find new friends?

Uncle Joe had suggested she get involved with the singles group at church, but who had time for that? Maybe she was meant to be the unmarried veterinarian, married to her animals. If so, what's so bad about watching old Westerns on TV with a man old enough to be her grandfather?

"Because you deserve more. I want so much more for you. All the good things life has to offer." Who was that? She didn't want to listen to that inner voice. She knew the truth. She didn't deserve all the good things the world has. She didn't really deserve to live. Her life was bought at the price of her mother's life. Nothing could change that.

Grace was continuing her efforts to wean Peanut. It wasn't going very well. One day a week was not enough. She needed to bconsistent. Every day. At this rate, Peanut would still be attached to his mother's teat at one. She'll never be able to train him. What was she thinking? Maybe it would be better if Abel sold the horses to someone who knew what they were doing.

"But no one will love them more than you do." That nagging voice again.

She planned on spending Saturday afternoon at the farm, working on weaning Peanut. She wasn't going to change her plans because of Abel. She would just avoid him.

Abel was a hard man to avoid. He came up to the fence around the corral as she struggled to get Peanut away from Lady.

"What are you trying to do?"

"What does it look like?"

"It looks like you're trying to get that colt away from his mother and failing miserably."

"That would be a pretty accurate assessment."

"Here. Let me help. That's a two-person job." Abel hopped over the fence and took hold of Lady's reins. "Whoa, Mama. No one's going to hurt your baby," he crooned into her ear while Grace pulled Peanut away and placed him in another corral on the other side of the barn.

"They say you need to keep them separate to wean horses. So far, every time I separate them, the minute Peanut sees his mother, he's right back nuzzling her. I don't know how I'm going to do this. I was hoping to get him weaned before the twins are born, but it's impossible. I need two large pens, close by, where he can see his mother but can't get to her. They also suggest a nanny for the foal, to keep them company, but Eleanor can't do it, not when she's expecting. I don't know what I'm doing." The more she talked the quicker the words came out of her mouth till she didn't know what she was saying.

"Whoa, slow down. Take it easy. Who says he has to be weaned at four months?"

"The experts. The books I'm reading. It says four to six months. I don't want to be weaning Peanut while taking care of Eleanor's twins." Grace could feel her face flush as she kept talking faster and faster.

"When is Eleanor due?"

"March. But twins could come earlier."

"Okay. Say they are born early March. Peanut won't be six months till April. What would be the harm of waiting till then?"

"But we don't know what we will run into with the twins."

"And if he's not weaned at six months, what would that hurt? That's assuming there are unexpected problems with the twins. Let's not expect the worse. Come April, it will be warmer. You can leave them outside all day and separate them into adjacent corrals."

"We don't have adjacent corrals."

"We don't now, but we will by April. If we have to, we can do abrupt weaning. Two days of intense work with the colt to get him over the initial loss, then we keep them separate for a month while Mama's milk dries up."

"We? And since when do you know so much about horses?"

"Since I spent my teen years here on this farm. Didn't my grandpa mention that?"

"No, but Seth did. Though he didn't say much about you."

"Maybe I can make up for that over dinner tonight. Fill you in on all my boring history."

"I'm not going."

"But you said you didn't have plans."

"Well, something came up."

"I just want to thank you for helping me out last weekend. What's the problem?"

"The problem is, you think I'm pathetic with nothing to do besides watch TV with an old man. Well, I'll have you know, I had a boyfriend, and a regular Saturday night date, till you sent him away."

"You talking about Seth?" Again, that look on Abel's face any time his brother was mentioned. A look she couldn't read.

"Yes, I am."

"Look, I don't think you're pathetic or need me to take you out. Let me show my gratitude by treating you to a nice dinner. Not a date. A business dinner."

Grace frowned.

"You know, I'm not used to asking more than once."

"Okay, as long as it's not a date." Grace agreed. It would be nice to go out, even if it was with Abel.

"Now, what is the nicest restaurant in town?"

"That would be Giglio's, the Italian restaurant downtown. But that's too expensive."

"You let me worry about that. But for now, I think we have a colt that really isn't ready to be weaned from its mother."

Peanut had been kicking the fence and whinnying the whole time they had been talking. Grace let him back into the corral with Lady. He ran up to her and nuzzled up to her belly.

"Horses are social animals. They don't like being alone," Abel commented. "You shouldn't have to do all of this alone," he added. "How about I pick you up at seven?"

"How about I meet you there at seven?" Grace countered. After all, it was a business dinner.

"That will work. See you then."

Just business.

Chapter 31

What to wear? Seth had taken her to casual places. The Burger Barn, Hot Diggity Dog, The Crab Shack. She didn't have any dressy clothes, just her church clothes. Didn't have a need for them. She opted for a dress that didn't cling to her body, exposing every lump of excess weight. She wasn't fat, but she wasn't model skinny either, like Ashley and Josie. If only she were taller. She had always been on the pudgy side as a kid. She had thinned out as she grew up but not as much as she wanted. Some would call her Rubanesque, back in the days when curves were appreciated. Or curvaceous, back when the term was a compliment. Her lab coat at work covered a multitude of sins, like extra cinnamon rolls or extra pieces of her grandma's pies.

She experimented with wearing her hair down, letting it fall naturally on her shoulders, then pinned it up into a bun. A step above her signature pony tail. She opted for low heels, not wanting to venture out into the ice and snow on heels, though she did glance longingly for a moment at her high heeled, strappy sandals. Those would have to wait till spring or summer. A little bit of make-up and she was ready, throwing on her good red winter coat. She hadn't worn it since Christmas Eve. It needed to be redeemed. She hoped this night would go better than that one.

Abel was already seated when she arrived. He stood up and pulled out her chair for her. She resisted admitting to herself how handsome he was in his cashmere sweater, tie and jacket. So different from Seth with his fair-skin and light hair. Abel's mustache nicely covered his lip, like some of the cowboys in the Westerns she had watched, like Tom Selleck or Burt Reynolds. Clearly, she was watching too many westerns.

"I ordered a bottle of wine for us. I hope that's okay."

"I don't drink."

"Oh, I guess I should have asked. I can have them cork the wine and take it home."

Grace looked at the glass sparking with red wine. It looked so pretty. "Maybe just a taste." She sipped and grimaced.

"It's an acquired taste. You don't have to drink it."

"No, that's okay. How can one glass of wine hurt?" She sipped again then pushed the glass away. "I guess it's not a taste I care to acquire."

"My grandmother didn't drink either, though I suspect she snuck a few snifters of brandy when Grandpa wasn't watching. Grandpa can be a challenge to live with."

"He's not bad. I'm fond of him."

"That's because he knows he can't order you around. He's still under the impression that he can order me and Seth around. He does that to every family member."

"Tell me about your mother. Your grandfather doesn't talk about her."

"That's because they are both bull-headed."

"Where is your mother now? Seth said something about her travelling the world with husband number three."

The waiter came to take their orders. Grace quickly scanned the menu and ordered the linguini in clam sauce.

"Very good. And for you sir?"

"I'll have the steak. Can't go wrong with a good steak, right?" he smiled at Grace.

"You were telling me about your mother."

"My grandfather cut off all ties with her when she was pregnant with me. He wanted her to have an abortion, didn't like my father. She refused, ran off with my father, but they never married. He left her shortly after I was born."

"Seth told me you have different fathers. But your last names are the same?"

"Seth's father, Richard Barton, adopted me when he married my mom. He was the closest I had to a father, him and Grandpa."

"What about your names? You and Seth have Biblical names. Was your mother religious?"

"That was my grandmother's doing. She was the churchgoer."

"I thought your mom had left her family before you were born."

"That was Grandpa. My mom still had contact with Grandma. She didn't know what name to give me, so Grandma suggested Abel. Abel was a farmer. 'He will need to be a hard worker, good with his hands,' Grandma had said. Then when Seth was born, Grandma named him for Adam and Eve's third son. 'He was a sweet boy,' she said."

And so he was, Grace thought. "Then that explains it."

"Explains what?"

"Why Seth doesn't believe in God."

"Is that what he said?"

"Well, not exactly that. He said he believes in a spiritual power greater than us, but not a personal God in Jesus."

"That sounds like him. Our mom didn't take us to church, but Grandma did her best to make up for it, cramming every bit of religion into us she could."

"Do you believe in God?"

"I guess I do. I have no reason not to believe, but I'm too busy to worry about God. Still all those years going to the Lutheran Church did some good."

"You attended the Lutheran Church in Cascade Falls? How come I never saw you?"

"Because we attended the Missouri Synod Lutheran Church. They are more conservative. You attend the ELCA church. My grandmother would have nothing to do with that church, said they were heretics and radicals."

"I never thought of myself as a heretic. And radical? I guess I don't see it."

"You would have liked my grandmother, and she would have eventually come around and accepted you even though you're a heretic."

"Do you attend church now?"

"No, not enough time. But enough about me. What about you? What about your mother?"

"My stepmom is a teacher. My mom died from cancer when I was two. Your mom refused to have an abortion and was disinherited. My mom refused to have an abortion when she was pregnant with me and lost her life. The doctor wanted her to have an abortion so they could aggressively treat her cancer but she refused to do that. They held off treatment until I was born."

"That doesn't mean she would have lived if they had started treatment earlier."

"She would have had a better chance."

"But then the world would have been deprived of wonderful you."

Grace looked down at her plate. Maybe she should try another sip of wine. She was relieved when the waiter came with their meals so she could end this discussion.

There was a moment of silence as each tried their meal. "Mmmmm, so good," Grace said as she slurped a long noodle. "How's yours?"

"It's steak. What's not to love?" Abel cut off a piece for her. "Try it."

"Mmmm, good." Grace allowed the juicy piece of meat to soften in her mouth as she slowly chewed. "But not as good as my linguini."

"I thought maybe you were a vegetarian. You know, animal rights and all."

"You can love animals and still like a good steak or burger."

"Good to know. Do you have a pet? Don't all vets have pets?"

"It's not good to have a pet if you don't have time to care for them. We had a dog, Lucky. He died when I was ten. After that, I wanted a dog, but it takes time to raise a dog. My dad and stepmom were busy working, my sister Ashley only thought about dance and then moved out at seventeen to go to New York. And Jacob, once he started playing basketball, that was all he wanted to do."

"Jacob Reese? The Golden State Warriors? Is he your brother?"

"Why so surprised?"

"You never said anything. You sure don't have his height."

"No, Jacob got all the height."

"You're a good five four or five, that's not so short."

"That's with my work boots on." Grace took another slurp of linguini. So good. "And then I started helping out at the vet clinic. My best friend, Josie — her mother was the vet there. She let me hang out and help with the animals. I did have one dog during high school. A pit bull. His owners weren't able to take care of him. The wife was in the hospital with a stroke and it was all the husband could do to take care of her. They were going to have him put to sleep but I figured he had a few good years left so I offered to take him. By the time he died, I had started college and then vet school. I didn't have time to take care of a dog. What about you?"

"Just like church, I don't have time for either. My business is pretty all consuming."

"That's too bad."

"The money's good." Abel shrugged. "Now that you are done with vet school, are you going to get a dog?"

"I still don't have time. I have your grandfather's horses." She tried another sip of wine. This time it went down easier.

"That's right. If you were to get a dog, what kind would you get? A Cocker Spaniel or a Foo-Foo dog like a poodle?"

Grace laughed. How little he knew her. "No, that's not me. Labs are good dogs, good temperament. Maybe a Golden Retriever. If I were to get a dog though, I'd get a rescue dog."

"St. Bernard?"

"No, a dog that has been rescued and needs a good home."

"That does sound like you."

"And what kind of dog would you want?"

"We used to have hound dogs, when I was a teen. Grandpa liked to hunt. We also had an Australian Shepherd. They're good with horses. If you had a dog, the dog could be a companion for Peanut while you wean him."

"So, this is a business dinner?"

"I have to find a way to justify it as a business expense." Abel's lip went up in his crooked smile as he took another bite of steak.

The meal went well. She enjoyed his company, but when he mentioned Sunday dinner, she balked. "It's not you, it's just you and my family."

"A little awkward, having me meet the whole family."

"Yes."

"But this isn't a date. Just a business meeting."

"My family won't see it that way."

A warm smile lit up his eyes. "Don't worry. I won't put you on the spot. It actually would be nice to leave earlier and avoid some of the traffic. As long as my grandfather is happy and in such capable hands, I think I'll leave before dinner tomorrow. You'll make my apologies to your family, won't you?"

"It isn't that I don't want you there."

"But you don't, and I'm okay with that. Some other time."

"Thank you. Now I owe you." She didn't understand why Seth thought Abel was so difficult. He was surprisingly reasonable, or was that the wine talking?

Chapter 32

Grace was getting used to the sound of heavy footsteps and a deep voice interrupting her work. She knew each of the three Blackburn men by the sound of their footsteps. Seth's had been light and easy, much like himself, sprinting, full of energy. Lamar's was slow and hesitant, testing the ground lest he slip, or testing his legs to make sure they would support him. But Abel's was steady and confident, just like him. His voice heavy and deep-throated — unlike Seth's whose voice was light and soft-spoken. Lamar's had the gravel sound that comes with age and wisdom. She loved all three footsteps for different reasons.

Lamar sometimes came out to the barn after dinner to check on her if she took what he considered to be too long, carrying a large flashlight to find his way and guide her back to the house.

"You know I can find my way back without you coming out. What I don't need is for you to slip and end up in the hospital again," she scolded. He ignored her words.

"A young lady shouldn't be walking alone in the dark."

Abel was in the habit of coming out to the corral on the weekend to watch her work with the horses.

"Just seeing what I'm paying for," he would say with a smile.

This time he seemed to have another agenda. "I need you at the house."

"But I'm not done."

"It can wait. Come now."

Grace frowned. What could be so important that it couldn't wait twenty minutes? Abel stood not budging, intractable. Was it worth the effort to fight him on this? She patted Lady on the rump. "Okay. I'll be there."

Grace was surprised when Abel didn't wait to walk with her. He usually accompanied her back to her car each Saturday when she was done. Instead he sauntered ahead of her, his long legs taking one step to her two.

The kitchen was empty when she got back to the house.

"We're in the living room," Abel called out.

Grace took off her boots and put them outside on the porch so as not to track mud from the barn into the house. Usually she had her tennis shoes waiting for her to slip on, but not on Saturdays. On Saturdays she kicked off the mud then drove home where her shoes awaited her in the garage by the door.

She quietly padded through the house in her socks till she entered the living room and was almost knocked over by a large, by her standards, hyperactive dog. The dog had long, reddish brown hair and a white chest and herded her towards Abel and Lamar.

"Who is this?" Grace squatted down and laughed as the dog licked her face. She estimated his weight at sixty pounds as she ran her hands over his body.

"Shep, down," Abel ordered. The dog backed away. "This, Dr. Reese, is your nanny for Peanut."

"My nanny?"

"Your companion animal for weaning Peanut. Shep's an Australian sheep dog. He's already trained to work with horses. You need help weaning Peanut. Now you have Shep."

"You knew about this?" Grace looked over at Lamar. He seemed just as pleased as Abel with the dog.

"Only found out about it this morning when Abel arrived with the dog, but I must say, he's one fine looking dog."

"I told you when I got a dog, I wanted a rescue dog." Grace gave Abel a guarded look.

"And your next dog will be a rescue. Shep is a working dog. He's already housebroken and trained. The ideas is not to add to your workload, but to help. A rescue dog would require attention.

Australian shepherds are one of the top breeds for working with horses."

Abel was right about the work required for rescue animals. There usually were issues, behavior problems, that needed to be addressed. Nothing she couldn't handle, but it would have been yet another demand on her time. "You seem to have thought of everything."

"Besides, he'll be added security at night when you're at the barn."

Was he implying walking from the barn at night? Like grandfather, like grandson. "Not that I need it, but thank you." A dog would be better than Lamar's shotgun for security. Could hardly blame Lamar, living out here alone. An old man could be an easy target. That didn't mean she liked it.

"Let's introduce Shep to the horses," Abel suggested.

All three walked to the corral. Shep was well trained. He made friends with the horses, but especially with Peanut, walking up to him and playfully nipping. Grace wondered how much he had cost. Money seemed to be no problem where the Barton boys were concerned. Each spent money freely, just on different things. She knew where Abel got his money. Didn't know where Seth got his. As far as she knew, he didn't have a source of income. Maybe his grandfather had been paying him to help with the farm. Or maybe he had saved money he had earned. He certainly wasn't independently wealthy. She doubted he would have stayed around Cascade Falls if that had been the case. Seth wasn't a big spender when it came to going out. For all his love of art and museums and poetry, his tastes ran more to less expensive fare than Abel. Grace didn't mind. She was more of a Burger Barn person than Giglio's. But he did enjoy going to local bars, mixing with "the regulars" and playing Keno. Wherever Seth went, he made friends. Abel, not so much. It took longer for him to warm up to strangers.

"Now that we have Shep, we can work on weaning Peanut. How about next weekend? I've been thinking. It's hard enough for an older mare to nurse one foal, much less two. Once Peanut is weaned, maybe Lady would help with the foals," Abel suggested.

"I've been thinking too." Grace leaned against the rail of the corral, watching Shep run among the horses. "I've been reading about natural methods for training horses, including weaning them. None recommend abrupt weaning. Too hard on the mare and the foal. Some even recommend waiting for nine months, more like foals were weaned in the wild."

"But what about Eleanor and the twins?"

"I've been thinking about that too. I've already started Peanut on creep feed. The more he eats, the less milk he will require. That will leave Lady with extra milk for the twins."

"Do you think that will work? Would Peanut have a problem with the new foals if they are drinking 'his' milk?"

"No more than he would if he had been abruptly weaned and separated from his mother. This might work better. We could wean all three of them together during the summer."

"You young people," Lamar shook his head. "Pampering these horses like they were babies. In my day, we separated the foals from the mares and that was that. None of this mollycoddling the horses. After two days, the foals were over the worst. After a month or two, we could let them back with their mothers."

"That was the practice back then, Lamar. Doesn't mean it was the best practice, or the worst, but times change. Horse trainers are trying different techniques now, ones that are more natural, more in tune with the horse's spirit," Grace said.

"It's worth discussing further," Abel said. "How about over dinner tonight? I hear there's a good steakhouse downtown."

"And expensive," Grace inserted.

"You let me worry about that. It's a business expense. What do you say, Grandpa? Doesn't a nice steak sound good?"

"Naw. I'll leave that to you young people. Besides, Mrs. Hill has already prepared me a dinner and left it in the refrigerator. A nice tasty chicken." The inflection in Lamar's voice left no doubt as to what Lamar thought about his dinner.

"Come on, Grandpa. You know you'd rather have a steak."

"Someone should stay with Shep on his first night in a new place. I'll be fine."

"Okay, then we'll bring you home a steak."

"Now that sounds good," Lamar agreed.

"So, Grace, steak place tonight. Do you want me to pick you up?"

"You know we don't have to go to such an expensive place. It might be easier to lay out plans at the Burger Barn."

"But I promised my grandfather a steak."

Grace knew when she was beat. "Okay, the steakhouse, tonight at seven. I'll meet you there."

Grace looked through her clothes again. She couldn't wear the same dress she wore last week. The options were slim. This had never been a problem with Seth. Maybe it was just that Seth didn't have the money to go to more expensive places.

She opted for her one classy dress, deep blue to bring out the blue in her eyes, a "stylish" cut, not that she knew anything about that. Her stepmom had said that when they had gone shopping.

"It's a classic style that never goes out of fashion." Ava had insisted on buying her a dress as a present when she graduated from college. When she graduated from vet school, Grace figured Ava had given up on her as there was no mention of another dress to hang unworn in her closet. Grace frowned at herself in the mirror as she struggled to pin her hair on top of her head in a loose bun.

"Do you want to borrow some of my jewelry?"

Grace jumped at her stepmother's voice. She didn't realize she had left the door to the bathroom open while fixing her hair.

"No, that's too much trouble."

"No trouble at all." Ava reached up and finished the bun for her. "If you're going to wear your hair up, you need the right earrings, dangling ones to draw attention to your beautiful complexion and high cheek bones." Ava disappeared, then came back with a set of earrings with dangling oval sapphires. "Perfect. Small and light. It's good to see you finally get some use out of that dress. Now, about your shoes."

Ava's disapproval was evident when she glanced at Grace's flat pumps. "I'm sure I have something more appropriate." Ava led her into her room where she rummaged in her closet.

"No high heels, Ava. I have to be able to walk."

"How about these?" Ava pulled out navy blue shoes with an inch heel. "Not too high, but enough to give you a little lift. Stylish, but not so stylish to say you are trying too hard. The right shoe complements and completes the ensemble."

Grace looked at the finished product in the full-length mirror. She preferred her work boots.

"It's not me."

"But it is you. Do you have any idea how pretty you are? Ashley isn't the only one in the family with good looks. You are both beautiful, just in different ways."

Grace didn't believe her, but it was too late to change out of the outfit. Not if she was going to be there by seven.

"It's just a business dinner. We are going to discuss how we want to go about weaning Peanut and other stuff related to the horses."

"No one says you can't look nice for a business meeting. Let's show your dad."

Grace held onto the stair railing as she adjusted to Ava's shoes. Ava was right. They were surprisingly comfortable. You can have style and comfort in the same shoe.

Her dad was in the living room watching TV. He looked up with an approving smile. "Who's the lucky man?"

"It's just Abel, and it's a business dinner."

"Sure." Her dad winked at Ava. She didn't care. She knew what it was. It was nice to get dressed up though.

Abel seemed to think so too as he smiled upon her approach. She made her way through the restaurant, self-conscience about his eyes watching her. If she had been Ashley, she would have accepted this as her right. Who didn't want to watch Ashley, how she looked and moved? Ashley naturally drew attention to herself. Not so much Grace. She was embarrassed by the attention.

"You look amazing," Abel said as he pulled out a chair for her.

"Not too dressy for a business meeting?"

"It's perfect. The only problem is all the young men who can't take their eyes off of you."

"Ha ha." She could count on her pinky the number of young men in the restaurant, and that man was clearly not interested in her as he gazed at the long-haired, long-legged blonde in a low-cut dress sitting across the table from him. No, this wasn't where the men her age congregated. That left only Abel, though he was clearly in his thirties. Not old, but older than her. Was he getting the wrong idea?

"You know, Seth and I were dating. We didn't break up when he left."

"Just business. The fact that it's at a nice restaurant with an attractive woman doesn't change that. It just makes the deal sweeter."

"Okay." Grace relaxed. What harm was there in this? Wasn't it good that she has a good relationship with Seth's brother and grandfather for when he gets back? Wouldn't Seth be happy to know she was getting along with his family? Not that he would know it, since he had neglected to call or text.

Grace pulled a notebook and pen from her purse.

"What's that for?" Abel asked.

"To take notes. This is business. Also, I wanted to talk to you about adding another corral. The current one isn't going to be big enough once we add two more horses."

"Order first. Then we can discuss business." Abel put his hand over hers on the notebook. Her hand felt warm and safe under his touch. She looked into his eyes and flushed as his hand remained over hers for a moment longer than necessary. Once her hand was freed, she set the notebook aside and fumbled for the menu.

156

"I'm getting a big juicy rib eye," Abel commented from behind his menu. "What about you?"

Grace studied the menu. She had been thinking fish. "Maybe the cod or shrimp."

"Who comes to a steakhouse and orders fish? You could get surf and turf." Abel looked over the menu as if preparing to order for her. "Or we can have shrimp appetizers. You have to at least try some steak. You can't go wrong with filet mignon."

Grace looked at the price. Even though she wasn't paying, she had a hard time at the thought of ordering one of the most expensive items on the menu.

"I'll have the New York strip steak, rare, loaded potatoes and asparagus," Grace told the waiter before Abel could intervene.

"And we'll have the shrimp cocktail appetizer," Abel added. "I also need a New York Strip Steak dinner, medium rare, to go, before we leave."

"Very good, sir." The waiter added the appetizer and extra dinner to their order before leaving.

"Now that that's done, let's talk business. I thought you wanted to bring Lady to the horse clinic in April. It will be hard to do that with Peanut tagging along."

"I thought about that. I thought maybe by then Peanut would be able to be separated from his mother for six hours or so. Just enough time for me to take Lady to the afternoon session."

"And if not?"

"If not, I guess I'll deal with that then."

"If we had a riding arena, we could host the clinic ourselves. Then Peanut and Lady wouldn't have to be separated for so long."

"That's an even bigger if. There's no way we can set up an arena in that short a time."

"If we did an outdoor one, we could."

"And if it rained?"

"We'd deal with that then."

Grace laughed. "The venue has already been set and advertised. I don't think we can change it now."

"Just a thought. I thought tonight was for dreaming big. Isn't that why you brought that notebook? We could sketch out our ideas for an arena and a training corral without corners."

"You've been doing your homework."

"You're not the only one studying these new methods for training horses."

"But I don't think your grandfather is interested. As far as I know, all he wants is a few horses on the farm. And last I knew you were planning on selling Peanut and the twins once they were old enough and trained. Why this sudden interest?"

"And last I knew you were going to help with the delivery of the twins, then you were going to be gone."

"That was the plan." When had that plan changed? Maybe about the same time Abel had changed. Or maybe he hadn't changed, just her perception of him had changed. Maybe when she realized he wasn't the cold-hearted business man who only saw dollar signs wherever he looked.

Grace was relieved by the arrival of the appetizers.

"We can talk more after dinner," Abel suggested. She tucked her notebook back in her purse. "Or not. I think we have discussed enough business to warrant calling this a business dinner."

Without business to talk about, the conversation waned. Grace played with her shrimp, dipping it in cocktail sauce and nibbling bites. What could they talk about that they hadn't already talked about?

The waiter placed a large platter in front of her, more than half taken up by the New York strip steak, oozing with blood. How was she going to finish that and still fit in her dress?

"When do you think Eleanor will be having her foals?" Abel asked in between bites of steak and potato.

"I thought we were done with business."

"This is pleasure." Abel smiled.

"She's not due for a couple of weeks, but with twins, it could happen earlier."

"Do you have help lined up?"

"Just Caroline."

"I'm going to try to take time off, but I can't promise. It all depends on what's happening at the factory." Abel looked at her as she attempted to make a dent in her steak. "You don't eat much steak, do you?"

"That obvious?"

"I'm sorry. I didn't mean to force you to eat something you don't like. You can order something else."

"No, it tastes great. It's just so big."

"That's what doggie bags are for." Abel took another bite of his steak. "Do you ride?"

"No. I tried once, but it didn't go well."

"Did you fall off?"

"No, nothing like that. I just couldn't get Eleanor to do what I wanted her to do."

"Once is not enough. You don't know what you are missing. I've seen you work with Lady. I'm sure you can do it. We can try tomorrow morning."

"You forget, I have church. What about you? How come you don't ride?"

"I used to. Used to be good at it too, or so I was told. Back when I was living with Grandma and Grandpa."

"What happened?"

"Nothing really. I moved away for college and never looked back."

"Why? You care about your grandfather. Why did you stay away all those years?"

"I guess I got caught up in making money. Got my MBA and CPA, then went into business for my current employer and worked my way up the ranks so that now I'm running one of his factories." Abel shrugged and took another bite of steak.

"What about relationships? Family? Don't you want a family?"

"I thought I did at one point. Didn't work out. I guess I'm married to my work. What about you?"

"I guess I'm married to my work too. Doesn't mean I don't want a family someday." Grace took one more bite of steak then put her fork down. "This is so good, but I can't finish it."

"Take it home with you. You can have steak and eggs for breakfast. Now, about dessert."

"None for me," Grace insisted.

"How can you turn down crème brûlée?"

"I believe I just did."

"You'll have some of mine."

Grace watched as the waiter lit the crème brûlée. It flamed, leaving a golden crust on top.

"It's worth it just for the pyrotechnics," Abel said, watching her rather than the flame. He insisted she try some. It was every bit as creamy good as he had said it would be. She found herself sneaking additional tastes until he finished it off.

"Next time, you get your own," he told her. "Now about those riding lessons. Next week. I'll have you up on Lady and riding in no time."

"We'll see," Grace said as Abel escorted her out, his hand lightly touching the small of her back. We'll see.

Chapter 33

Grace scanned her appointments. Mr. and Mrs. Peterson were coming in at ten. Had they gotten a new pet?

"I see that the Petersons are scheduled today. Did they say why?" she asked Adah. It wasn't like her to not note the reason for the visit.

"Routine check-up."

"For who?"

"Priscilla."

"Really?" Sure enough. Come ten o'clock both Petersons came in. Mr. Peterson proudly carried Priscilla.

"When I last saw Priscilla, she wasn't doing well. What happened?" Their vet tech did follow up phone calls on patients. She must have missed something.

"You tell us. It must be what you gave her did the trick. That or she used one of her nine lives to stay with us," Mrs. Peterson said.

"And you weren't doing well either." Grace looked at Mr. Peterson, as spry as ever, just like Priscilla.

"Seems we both got better." Mr. Peterson smiled at the cat in his arms. "Neither of us were ready to leave just yet."

"That's a good thing," Mrs. Peterson reached over and petted Priscilla. "Don't know what I would do without both of them."

Priscilla was robust, had even put on weight. Clearly she must not have gotten into any antifreeze. No cat recovers from ingesting antifreeze. Grace was glad to be proven wrong. She was always glad to be proven wrong when it came to death.

"It appears Priscilla has a lot more years ahead of her." Grace gave the cat her vaccinations. "I don't know what you are doing, but keep doing it."

"We will. Thank you, Doctor." Mrs. Peterson held the door for her husband as he carried out the fully recovered pet.

Grace felt her phone vibrate in her lab coat pocket. Seth? She stepped into her office to take the call.

"Have you gotten any of my texts?"

Grace was barely able to make out the words over the static on the line. "Texts? What texts? I haven't received any."

"I've been sending them. I guess that's why you didn't respond. I thought maybe you were ghosting me."

"Why would I do that?"

"I didn't know what my brother's been telling you about me."

"He hasn't said much."

"You're breaking up. What did you say?"

"I said, he hasn't said much."

"Sorry. I still can't hear."

"Where are you?"

No response. She had lost the call. Wherever he was, the connection wasn't good. He must be somewhere with limited phone access. Maybe in the middle of the Pacific. Or some jungle. Seth wasn't one to stay put for long. She did know that much about him, based on all of the stories he had told her about his travels. Maybe it was just as well. She wasn't one to travel the world, though there was that stint in Africa during the summer between her second and third year in vet school. It had been a chance to observe African animals in the wild and get practical experience with exotic wildlife in case she was interested in working at a zoo or animal preserve. She had enjoyed the experience but it had confirmed for her that exotic animals were not where her interest lay. She was much more interested in pets and domestic animals and their owners.

She looked at Seth's number. If only she could figure out where he was calling from. Then at least she would have an idea what he was doing. What did Seth think Abel might be telling her? What was it about the Barton brothers? Why couldn't they get along? She didn't know, but she knew someone who might.

"What's up with Seth and Abel?" she asked Lamar over dinner. While Lamar often talked about himself and his past, he rarely talked about his daughter or grandsons.

"What do you mean? Who have you been talking to?"

"No one. Or actually, Seth called today but it wasn't a good connection."

"It's never a good connection where Seth is concerned. Some things are better left unspoken."

"But why?"

"Who knows what goes on between brothers. Just because two people are raised in the same family doesn't mean they have to like each other, or have anything in common."

Grace thought about Ashley. She guessed he was correct there, whether talking about brothers or sisters.

"And what about their mother, your daughter, Maggie? How come she never visits?"

"You aren't going to let this be, are you?"

"Not till I get satisfactory answers."

"Then I guess it will continue to bother you because I don't have any satisfactory answers for you. Now don't you think you need to be looking after those horses?"

"This isn't over, old man." Grace cleared her plate.

"I wouldn't expect it to be. You're not one to give up easily." Lamar cleared his plate. "I'll take care of these dishes. You get on with your work." He sent her out the door.

Grace walked to the barn with Shep by her side. Shep quickly took to his duties, staying with the horses all day, sleeping in her room at night, though at times she would wake up and hear him patrolling the house.

True to her word, Grace continued to ask Lamar about his family, and he continued to evade her questions. Seth was unavailable. That left Abel, but he was as reticent to talk about his mother and brother as his grandfather. She determined she would ask him when he came next weekend.

Abel came up behind her and threw a saddle on the fence. "Time for your riding lesson."

"I told you I don't ride."

"And I told you I would teach you. It will be good for Lady."

"Caroline rides her."

"Why should she have all the fun? You have to try."

Did she? Grace wanted to resist, but figured it wasn't worth the effort to fight Abel on this. She found herself climbing onto Lady with Abel's help. Maybe he was right. Maybe she should give it another try.

"What about Peanut?"

"We're just going to walk her around the corral for a while. Let's put Peanut in the side corral with Eleanor and Shep. He'll be fine. It will be good for him."

Grace held tight as Abel led Peanut out of the corral. Lady pulled to be with her colt. "Don't you think you should have moved Peanut before I got on Lady."

"You'll be fine." Abel saw Caroline come out of the barn where she had been cleaning out the stalls. "Here, take Peanut."

Grace was even less sure this time than the first time. Something about not knowing anything back then made it easier. She knew Lady wasn't going to buck her off or run away with her. But would the mare let her direct her?

"Riding a horse badly is easy. Anyone can get on a horse and ride, but to do it well it takes time and effort. You can't learn if you only ride now and then," Abel instructed her. "It's like ballet. Your sister didn't learn ballet overnight."

That she didn't. Grace remembered all of those years of practice. "Why are you telling me this now, while I'm on Lady. Wouldn't it have made more sense to warn me before I got up here."

"Not a warning. I just want you to not expect it to be easy or quick. That was your problem the last time. You got on and took off. You can do that, but you pick up a lot of bad habits that way that will be hard to unlearn. Better to take your time from the start. That was always Seth's problem. He didn't want to take the time or have the discipline to learn. He wanted to hop on and ride."

Abel took the reins and led Lady around the corral. "Just get the feel for it. Learn how to balance. It takes muscles to do that." Was that why she had felt like she was in a blender that first time, being bounced around? Was it because she hadn't been sitting right? Grace had read about riding in her horse books, but reading about something and actually doing it — very different.

"If all we do today is walk around the corral while you learn to balance and direct Lady, that will be enough."

Grace nodded. She could handle that. Abel showed her how to hold the reins and how to let Lady know when she wanted to turn left or right. After an hour Grace was feeling sore as she struggled to balance. Her legs were shaky and she couldn't breathe when Abel helped her off Lady. He caught her as she stumbled, holding her upright until she was ready to stand on her own. Her head swam for a moment, then leveled out as she regained balance on firm ground and caught her breath.

"How about lessons for me?" Caroline asked.

"Sorry. I've seen you ride. You are already beyond my skill level." Abel handed Lady's reins to Caroline. "So, dinner tonight?" he asked Grace.

Grace was still unsure of her balance. "Sure, but this time I pick the place. Some place not so fancy."

"You don't like fancy?"

Grace tilted her head and raised her eyebrows. "How little you know me."

"Okay. That's fair. Before you leave, I want you to come up to the house."

Grace agreed. What did he have this time? Certainly not another dog. She finished with the horses then went up to the house. Abel and his grandfather were in the living room, Abel sitting on a large yoga ball.

"What are you doing?"

"This is for you." Abel rolled the ball over to her. "If you're to get good at riding, you need to develop your muscles. Ideally you should be riding at least twice a week, but I don't want you riding alone yet. During the week you can practice by sitting on this yoga ball. It will help you develop the core muscles you need. Try it."

Grace sat and bounced.

"Don't bounce, balance," Abel instructed her. "You can do it while watching *The Virginian*."

"The boy's right about the importance of building your muscle memory," Lamar said. "Riding every day is the best way. That's how I taught Abel here. We didn't have 'yoga' balls back then, but I guess it might work. Won't hurt."

"Did you teach Seth that way too?"

"Seth never had the patience for it. But Abel here, he was a natural, after two years of lessons."

Grace thanked Abel and made arrangements to meet him at the Burger Barn at seven that night. This time getting ready was easy, jeans and a denim shirt and boots. No fuss about jewelry or stylish shoes. Ava looked disappointed when she came down the stairs. Her dad just smiled.

"Going to the Burger Barn. I won't be late," she said on her way out the door.

"Won't matter if you are," her dad called after her. "It's not like you have a curfew."

She loved her parents, but living with them, having them know her comings and goings?

The Burger Barn was crowded with young people and their noise. They were lucky to find a booth. Grace could tell Abel was not used to the noise and commotion which was the Burger Barn on a Saturday night.

"You hate it here."

"No, no, it's all right," Abel said.

"Don't lie to me."

"Okay, it is awfully noisy. How can you have a conversation," he shouted above the noise.

"Don't worry. The teenagers will be clearing out soon to go to the dance at the high school. Then it'll just be us 'older adults.' It won't be as loud."

On schedule, the teens departed, leaving the room half empty, creating a vacuum as if all of the energy had been sucked out of the air when they left.

"Better?" Grace asked.

"Yes, but now it's too quiet."

"Is there any pleasing you?"

"I'm not hard to get along with. I only want one thing."

"And what's that?"

"My way." He smiled.

"You don't want much."

"Oh, I want a lot but my needs are few. I know how to go without."

Their waitress came to get orders. Abel ordered the bacon double cheeseburger, fries and a beer. She ordered the burger deluxe, light on the mayo, and a side salad.

"No fries?" the waitress asked.

"No fries." Grace handed her the menu.

"And an order of onion rings to share," Abel added as he handed over his menu.

"Not exactly what you are used to," Grace commented.

"You forget. I grew up here. I used to be part of that high school crowd, coming here before and after games and dances."

"But what are you doing here now? Why the riding lessons, the yoga ball? Why do you care? And don't say it's business."

"Okay. I won't say it, though it is." Abel sat back and sighed. "I think, the farm, this town, you. You're all reminders that there is more to life than work. Something I forgot ten years ago. It's nice to have something else to think about besides just work."

"So, me, the farm. We're a hobby for you?"

"I wouldn't say that."

"Then what would you say?"

Abel leaned forward and smiled. "A challenge. And I like challenges."

Their burgers arrived, forcing Abel to sit back. Grace happily sunk her teeth into the messy bun, mayo dripping from the bun onto her hands. So much for light mayo. She wiped her fingers clean then watched Abel tackle his burger, cheese dripping off the sides.

"Is it everything you remember?"

"That and more." He wiped his hands. "Every bit as greasy and good as when I was a kid."

Grace took another bite. This time the sloppy mixture dripped down the side of her mouth.

"Here, let me." Abel reached over to wipe away the mayo on the corner of her lip.

Grace looked away from him, then picked up her burger again. "Tell me more about Seth. What was he like when you were growing up?"

Abel shrugged and leaned back. "What do you want to know?"

"Everything."

"Everything? Now who wants too much?"

"Okay. You don't have to start with everything. How about the horses? You said Seth wasn't good with the horses."

"No, he was an impatient kid. Didn't want to work too hard. He was always chasing off after the next adventure. He loved horse riding at first, until he didn't. Until he discovered it required work."

"He learned how to play piano. That requires discipline and practice."

Abel put down his burger and munched a fry. "A lot of things did come easy for him. School. He got by with little work. And people. He was always popular."

"And you?"

"Not so much. I worked hard for every grade I got. I was popular enough. Played football. Girls like football players."

"Some girls."

"Not you?"

Grace shrugged. "They weren't interested in me."

"Then they were fools." Abel reached for an onion ring. "No, everything came easy for Seth, which is why it all ended up being too hard."

Grace frowned. "Huh?"

"I mean he never had to work at anything so he never learned to work."

"That sounds a lot like my brother."

"The basketball player? He has to work hard. It isn't just about talent."

"No. He does work hard now, but it took him a while to find what was worth working for. Maybe Seth hasn't found that yet."

"Maybe. Maybe he never will." Abel shrugged and reached for another onion ring. "Enough about my brother. How's Shep working out?"

"Wonderfully."

"Worth my investment then. And Eleanor. I'm wondering if Eleanor is as close to foaling as you indicated. Do you think you need to start staying over on the weekends, just till the twins are born?"

"I've been thinking about Eleanor too. We've been fortunate that she has gone this long without losing the foals. Twin deliveries are rare in horses. Horses, when they give birth, it's different from other farm animals. Once they go into labor it's pretty intense. Most foals are delivered within thirty minutes. They need to deliver within an hour or you lose the foal. Fortunately, most mares deliver without problem. But in the one percent of deliveries where there is a problem, you only have a short period of time to correct it. With twin deliveries the chances of problems more than double."

"What are you thinking?"

"I'm thinking, at the first sign of Eleanor being ready to deliver, maybe we should transport her to an equine surgery center. That way if there are problems, they will be able to take care of them right away. If we wait until Eleanor is in labor and there's a problem, we won't have time to drive the hour to the nearest surgery center. That way, if she needs a C-section, they will be able to save the foals and Eleanor."

"And if not?"

"We could lose all three horses."

"That is a consideration. I don't know that my grandfather will go for that."

"He will if you help me convince him."

"Speaking of which." Abel's phone rang. "Hi, Grandpa. We were just talking about you …" Abel paused as he listened. "Okay …" Another pause. Abel's face was no longer smiling. "Okay …" Abel put his free hand on the side of his face as he listened. "We'll be right there."

"What's wrong?"

"Grandpa said Shep was acting funny. Led him to the barn and didn't want him to leave. He thinks Eleanor may be getting ready to foal. Said to bring you back with me."

"Let's go." Grace stood up, leaving her half-eaten burger.

"Wait. He said we didn't need to rush, just don't 'lollygag,' as he says. We can finish our meals."

"Did you hear anything I just said? If Eleanor is getting ready to go into labor this is an emergency."

"But we don't know that."

Grace sat back down but didn't take another bite.

"You aren't going to finish your burger, are you?"

Grace shook her head. "And you wouldn't either if you cared at all for Eleanor."

Abel waved to the waitress.

"Do you want a takeout bag?" the waitress asked.

"No, that's okay. We need to leave." Abel gave her two twenties, enough for the meal and a substantial tip. "It's a good thing you chose this restaurant. So much easier to eat and run," he commented as they left the building. Grace didn't respond. Multiple scenarios were playing out in her head.

"See you there," Abel said as they climbed into their respective cars. Grace didn't respond. She was too busy planning for what might lay ahead.

Chapter 34

Grace rushed to the barn without stopping for her work boots.

Lamar met her at the barn. "I thought you might need these." He handed her work boots to her. She slipped off her dress boots and exchanged them for the other boots. She could see Eleanor pacing in her stall.

"Sure looks like she's getting ready," Lamar said as Grace approached Eleanor and felt her teats. They were swollen with milk and sticky with colostrum. Grace showed Abel her sticky fingers when he arrived.

"She's producing milk. She could go into labor any time now. Get the truck and trailer ready," she ordered.

"Wait, why do you need the trailer?" Lamar asked.

"Because Eleanor may go into labor any time now and if we wait it may be too late to get her to the surgery clinic."

"Who said anything about surgery? She hasn't even gone into labor yet."

"And if we wait and there's a problem, we won't have time to get her there. We are trying to save all three of your horses, so get out of our way." Even Grace was surprised at how strong she sounded. Usually she was the peacekeeper, trying to make sure everyone was heard and could come to an agreement. But not where an animal's life was concerned. She would save Eleanor and her babies and worry about the cost later.

"You heard her," Abel told his grandfather and left to get the trailer ready.

Grace called the surgery center. "I've got a mare about to deliver twin foals."

"How soon can you get here?"

"We'll be there in an hour."

"Is the horse in labor yet?"

"No." Grace walked over to the agitated mare and rubbed her side. "Hold on, Eleanor. Don't go into labor yet," she whispered. Eleanor responded by laying down on her side. "She just laid down," she told the vet tech on the phone.

"It sounds like she may be going into labor."

"She is. What should I do?"

"If she's already in labor it might be too late to save the foals by the time you get here. See if she is able to deliver them and if not, call us back. At least we can save the mare. We'll contact the on-call surgeon and alert him to the situation."

"The trailer's ready," Abel said as he entered the barn.

"We don't need it. At least not yet. It's too late. Eleanor is already in labor."

"What do you want me to do?"

"Hopefully Eleanor will do it all herself, but if not, get my kit out of my car … and Lamar, get some water."

"Then what?"

"We wait and pray," Grace said as she knelt beside the mare and massaged her stomach. "Then we give the mama a chance to do what she needs to do." Strong muscles pulsed throughout the horse's body. Finally a pair of hooves emerged, one ahead of the other.

"That's a good sign," Grace said. "The foal's presenting head first." Grace reassured Eleanor as she carefully reached to guide the foal through. "You don't want to pull if you don't have to. There's a danger of hurting the mare if you do that."

"Half way there," Grace said as head and shoulders emerged. With a push the foal came out onto the ground. "You can help clean up this foal a mite. Usually the mare licks her baby clean, but this mama has more work to do." Grace showed Abel how to wipe mucus out of the foal's nose to help it breathe. Eleanor was sweating profusely from the hard work. Grace wiped the sweat. Eleanor was laying quietly, resting, then she lifted her head in search of her baby.

"You aren't done yet, Eleanor." Grace continued to rub her body down. Then she felt the rise of muscle as contractions started again. "Here we go girl. You're doing fine," Grace reassured the horse and herself.

One hoof appeared. Grace looked for the second. It appeared to be facing up rather than down like the first foal. Hard to tell. When a second hoof didn't appear despite Eleanor's straining, Grace put on gloves, lubricated her hands and reached in. The second hoof was stuck, unable to push through into the vaginal canal. She needed to dislodge it. She reached up and realized the foal was in breech position. Sometimes you could repel the legs back inside and reposition the foal. Sometimes if you got the mare up and walking the foal would reposition on its own. This wasn't one of those times. She smelled death. She needed to get the foal out. Eleanor was getting weak. She kept straining. Grace could tell she was giving all she had.

"Is there a problem?" Abel asked.

"Breech birth."

"Can you reposition the foal?"

"Too late. Eleanor is weak. We're running out of time."

"What can we do?"

Good question. Grace knew what Lamar had said all along. If there were any problems, save the foals, not the mare. But she needed to do what was best for both mother and foal.

She looked over at the first foal, a small colt. He would need his mama's colostrum and as much of her good milk as he could get to grow strong. Often with twins, one is larger than the other. It appeared the large one was still inside Eleanor. Would she be able to push it out?

Grace listened to Eleanor's heartbeat. It was racing. Was the foal already gone? She checked her watch. How many minutes has Eleanor been in labor?

Eleanor was in distress. Grace laid her head against the swollen stomach, trying to sense the life inside, looking for answers. She looked at Eleanor. Eleanor's eyes pleaded with her as she gave a feeble push, nothing close to what would be needed to push the foal out. Grace knew what she needed to do.

"Abel, get my surgery kit out of my car. It's in the trunk."

Abel stood up from where he had been tending to the colt. Without a word he did what she commanded.

Grace pulled out her phone and gave it to Lamar. "Call Jill, the other vet at the clinic. Tell her what's happening and ask her to come as soon as she can."

Grace knew she could count on Jill. Jill had more experience with horses. But there was no way she could wait for her. She had to act and she had to act now. She didn't have the fifteen to twenty minutes it would take for Jill to get dressed and drive here.

She took her surgical kit from Able. "I need water."

"Already got it." Abel pointed to a filled bucket.

Grace looked through the shiny tools. She had never done this before. Now most surgeries are done in antiseptic clinics. But then James Herriot and other vets of his time routinely performed emergency surgeries in the field without the benefit of modern technology and methods. She picked up a scalpel, put her hand on Eleanor's abdomen and prayed. "God, guide my hands." Those were the only words she could manage. But they must have been enough for she cut deftly and swiftly, penetrating through layers of skin and muscle, pulling them back till she reached the womb. A slice revealed a hooded face resting on two hoofs. She reached in and pulled the foal out, passing it into Abel's waiting arms.

"See if you can get him breathing," she told Abel. Was she too late? Were all her efforts for nothing?

She set about sewing back together the folds of skin, all the while praying that Eleanor was okay. She heard a snort from the foal as it took in a deep breath, but nothing from Eleanor. She was weak, barely breathing but not moving. She showed no interest in her foals. Grace diverted her attention back to the foals. Abel was cleaning the second one, a filly, same coloring as her mother. The first was standing. Grace looked back at Eleanor. The mare lay still as she finished the sutures.

"How can I help?" Jill's voice broke through the fog in her head.

"It's too late." Grace stood up, in shock. Eleanor wasn't moving, wasn't breathing. She had killed her. "It's my fault. I should have known better. I thought I could do it by myself. I should have called you sooner. I should have taken Eleanor to the horse surgery clinic before this, where an experienced surgeon could have saved her." Grace started to sob.

Jill gently pushed Grace aside. "Here. Let me take over. You're exhausted."

Abel pulled her away from Eleanor and wrapped his arms around her as she cried. He stroked her hair and rubbed her shoulders much as she had massaged Eleanor. It didn't help. She cried harder.

"It's all right. Everything will be all right. It isn't your fault," he repeated in a soothing tone.

"No, it isn't all right." Grace continued to cry.

Abel hugged her. "It's not your fault. These things happen. What can I do to convince you of that?"

"But it is my fault. I killed her." Abel continued to hold her tight, keeping her from falling.

"I think there's someone here who would beg to differ," Jill called to her.

Grace wiped the tears from her eyes in order to see. What she saw was Eleanor licking her babies.

"She's weak, but she's going to make it," Jill assured her. "Let them rest for a while. Eleanor is exhausted."

"So are you." Abel hugged her again. "Grace, you were wonderful. Amazing."

Grace started laughing. She didn't feel so amazing. Then she started crying again.

"Grace, what's wrong?" Abel pulled away and looked at her.

"I don't know. I'm just so tired. And we aren't done yet. We have to make sure Eleanor is okay. Make sure she delivers the placenta. And the foals. We have to make sure there is enough milk for them. And colostrum."

"We will, but will you give yourself a break? Grace — do you have any idea how amazing you are?" Abel continued to look at her, his hands on either side of her arms, his eyes locked on hers.

"I don't feel amazing."

"You are, you and those amazing hands." Her hands were bloody from the surgery. She hadn't had a chance to clean them yet. Abel wiped her hands clean then lifted them up to his lips and kissed them. Tears flowed down her face.

"Grace, you did it. You saved those horses' lives. Why are you crying?"

"I don't know. I just am. Can't I just cry?"

"Of course you can, you crazy, wonderful woman." Abel hugged her till her shoulders stopped convulsing from the sobs. "Do you have any idea how crazy I am about you?" He whispered into her hair. Grace felt his warm lips on hers, amidst the stream of tears. She felt herself kiss him back. Wait. What was she doing?

She pulled away and wiped her face. That was wrong. "Eleanor, I have to check on Eleanor. We have to make sure she's okay and feed the foals."

"Mama and foals are just fine," Jill said with a laugh. The foals had found their mama's teats and were sucking contentedly.

Mama and the foals were okay. Why wasn't she?

Chapter 35

Grace recognized the sound of Abel's footsteps. He was staying the week to help with the care of the foals. The foals required constant attention. He took care of them during the day while she was at work. They shared the overnight responsibilities. As soon as she got home from the clinic she went to the barn, not stopping to even change her clothes. She did that before dinner. Then she was out with the horses again.

The week was a blur. She liked it that way. No time to think about Saturday night or that kiss.

"You know, as long as I'm here, there's no reason why you can't ride Lady, get in more practice. There's still enough light. You can get in a short lesson before dinner."

"Can't. Too tired. Besides I have to check on the foals."

"They're fine. That's what you've got me for." Abel waited for her to respond. When she didn't, he continued. "Grace, what's wrong? Did I do something wrong, because if I did, I'm sorry."

"You didn't do anything wrong."

"Then why are you acting this way? I thought we were getting along, but ever since Saturday night, you've been different, distant." Grace turned away from him. "If it's about that kiss, I don't apologize. I guess I was caught up in the moment. But I'm not sorry about it. I've wanted to kiss you since the day I met you."

"Really?" Grace turned to face him. "You sure have a strange way of showing it. You weren't exactly friendly the first few times we met."

"Okay, so it took me a while to recognize it. Doesn't mean it wasn't there." Abel frowned as Grace turned back away. "Now what's wrong?"

"You know I'm dating Seth."

"But you love me."

"How do you know that? What makes you think you know me? Know who I love?" This time when she faced him, she could feel her face flush with anger.

"Because I do." He put his hands on her shoulder, keeping her from turning away from him. "I know you, Grace Reese. I love you. And I believe you love me too. You may not realize it, but you do."

"Pretty cocky, aren't you?"

"Some say that's one of my most endearing qualities. Besides, like I said, I like challenges."

For a moment Grace thought he was going to kiss her again. Instead he let her go.

"So how about you hop on Lady for a short lesson. It will get your mind off of everything else."

Get her mind off of everything else, including him. That was a good idea.

Chapter 36

Grace heard two sets of feet approaching. Couldn't be Abel. He had stayed for most of the week to help with the foals. She was glad when an emergency at work forced him to leave on Friday. Glad for the time alone. Neither said another word about the kiss, but it was ever-present in her mind, only pushed aside by her work. It kept her awake at night as she tried to sleep knowing he was just down the hall from her.

"We figured if we wanted to see you, we had to come to you." She turned around and saw her grandmother followed by Peter.

"Besides, we wanted to see those twins," Peter added.

"There they are." Grace pointed to where the twins and Peanut frolicked in the corral alongside Eleanor and Lady. They had quickly formed a family group. She had kept Eleanor in her stall most of the week. The weekend was Eleanor's first chance to stretch her legs. She slowly moved about the pen, munching on bits of grass wherever she could find them. Lady had adapted to nursing the two additional foals. Peanut had complained at first, but was adapting as well, eating more grains and demanding less milk. The twins were close to being out of the danger zone. The first two weeks were crucial, requiring extra care and attention. They had successfully passed the first week. They were both small and not fully developed at the time of their birth, but were making up for it, nursing hungrily at both mares' teats.

"Beautiful," her grandmother said as she leaned on the fence. "Where's Abel? We thought he would be here. Give us a chance to meet this mystery man."

"He had to go back to Chicago. Some work emergency."

"I know how that can be," Peter said. "Who's helping with the foals?"

"Caroline. She helps after school and on the weekends. With her help and Lamar's, we are managing."

The three stood and marveled at the awesome sight of mares and foals.

"Since you couldn't come to Sunday dinner, we brought Sunday dinner to you." Her grandmother nodded at Peter. "Peter, get that food out of the car and take it to the kitchen." She waited till Peter was on his way before adding, "Quite the miracle. You did well."

Grace didn't respond.

"What's wrong?"

What was wrong? Did she dare tell her grandmother? If not her, who could she talk to? "It's just … when I saw the foal was in breech position, I couldn't bear the thought of letting her die. Other vets would have figured the second foal wasn't going to make it, was probably already gone. They wouldn't have risked the mother's life by performing a C-section. Especially not when Eleanor was so clearly under stress."

"What other option would they have had?"

"They could have done a fetotomy where you cut the dead foal into smaller parts to make delivery possible."

"But not you."

"No, I just couldn't take the chance that she was still alive. I had to try to save her, even at the risk of losing Eleanor."

"Now you know how your mother felt about you." Her grandmother spoke quietly, gently putting her arm around her.

"Maybe." Grace took a breath and looked at the grazing mare. "When I thought Eleanor had died …"

"But she didn't."

"No, I was lucky."

"Maybe there was more to it than that. Maybe you are more skilled than you realize." Her grandmother continued to hold her as they both looked at the miracles that were the horses.

"It wasn't me. I prayed and God guided my hands."

"Then what's the problem?"

"If God saved Eleanor and her foals, why didn't God save my mom? God could have." Grace turned to face her grandmother as she sought answers in her grandmother's face.

Her grandmother stared across the fields. "I wish I had an answer for you. I've asked that question many times. At the death of my brother and the death of my first husband, your grandfather. Far greater minds than mine have asked the same question with no answer. Sometimes these things happen. But now you know why your mom couldn't do anything to risk your life."

Grace didn't answer at first, looking down at the ground. Knowing that didn't help her. "Sometimes things happen. That's what Abel said when we thought Eleanor had died. It didn't help me feel better."

"Sometimes they do. Who knows the ways of God? I asked that question after your mom died too. Why would God take someone so good? Why would God leave you children without a mother? I don't have an answer — but I do know, God heals our wounds and hears us in our grief. You never completely get over, but you get on and you learn to live and love again."

"I can't talk to Dad about this. It upsets Ava."

"You can talk to me any time. Your mother loved you. A mother's love is a powerful love."

"And I missed out on that."

"No, you had it for two years." Her grandmother shook her head. "In those two years your mother poured out more love than some people experience in a lifetime."

"You think so?"

"I know so. And then you had your Aunt Kathleen, Grandma Mary and me to mother you. Then along came Ava. I think you've had more mothering than any girl can tolerate."

"It can be overwhelming at times. All these women looking out for you. You can be pretty bossy."

"As I have a right to be. The only love more powerful than a mother's love is a grandmother's love — and that you have in abundance."

Grace smiled but continued to look away.

"Is something else wrong?" her grandmother asked.

"Yes." Grace closed her eyes as she wondered what to say. "Abel kissed me."

"About time," her grandmother responded.

"But I'm dating Seth."

"Last I checked there was no ring on your finger." Her grandmother pointed at her hand. "Do you love Seth?"

"I thought I did. Now I don't know. Abel is so … bossy. Sometimes he orders me around like I'm an employee."

"Technically, you are."

"Yeah, I guess." Grace shook her head. "Seth is fun. He makes me laugh and he says all the right things."

"And Abel?"

"I don't know. At first, I didn't like him at all, but he isn't so bad after all."

"That's not much of a recommendation."

"I didn't mean it that way." Grace looked across the pasture. "He's kind and generous. He really cares about his grandfather."

"And Seth doesn't?"

"Sometimes I wonder. Seth has all the right words …"

"The right words don't mean anything if they aren't followed up by action."

Her grandmother was right. Grace didn't answer.

"And Abel is here, while Seth is who-knows-where."

"He's coming back. He told me."

This time it was her grandmother who didn't respond. "Well, I best see what Peter is up to. How about I warm up your dinner? Will you be done shortly?"

"I can be. I'll be up in few. Oh, and Grandma …" Grace stopped her grandmother before she left and gave her a hug. "Thank you. What would I do without you?"

"Oh, you'd manage, just not as well. And you wouldn't eat as well either."

Grace let go of her and watched as her grandmother walked the well-worn path to the farmhouse.

Chapter 37

Later that night, Grace relaxed in the overstuffed chair, a book on horses open in front of her. She put the book down when she saw the text message.

"Face time?" Josie. She hadn't talked to Josie for a while. So tired.

"Sure," she texted back. "I'm going upstairs," she told Lamar.

"So early?"

"I've got to be up to check on the twins." Grace excused herself and went into her bedroom before calling Josie.

"I was beginning to think you had run away with Seth." The face of her best friend appeared on the phone.

"Busy. The foals were born last weekend."

"And you couldn't take a moment to let me know."

"Sorry."

"How are they?"

"They're good, doing great."

"Then what's wrong?"

What had her face told her friend? If she couldn't talk to Josie, who could she talk to? "Abel kissed me."

"And that's a problem …?"

"Yes."

"If this is about Seth, I'd say, what's wrong with dating someone else while he's gone? He certainly doesn't seem to be too worried about keeping in touch with you."

"It isn't just about Seth. It's also about Abel."

"Why? You like him, don't you?"

"I don't know. At first, I didn't, but now …"

"Now is all that matters. If you like him now, what's wrong with getting to know him better?"

"Nothing, I guess."

"Grace, you've got two attractive brothers interested in you. Other women would be happy, but not you. When Seth was around, you weren't sure about him. Now that Seth is gone and Abel is around, you aren't sure about Abel. What is keeping you from giving in to love?"

What was keeping her? "Enough about me. You know what I've been doing. What have you been up to?" Grace changed the subject. Josie didn't challenge her on it this time.

After Grace ended the facetime with Josie, she saw she had a text from Abel.

"Call me."

She hesitated, then called. After all, he was her "boss."

"Hi, Abel. I was getting ready for bed."

"I just wanted to know how the foals were doing. I'm sorry I didn't call sooner. It's been crazy at the factory."

"The foals are doing good."

"I'm going to try to get away as soon as possible so I can help while you're at work. If not tomorrow, at least by Wednesday."

"That's no problem. My grandma and Peter are going to help your grandfather with them during the day."

"But what about nights?"

"I've got that covered."

"Then who's going to help you?"

Grace laughed. "I guess that would be me. I help myself." That I do, she thought as she hung up. But was it enough?

Chapter 38

By Thursday when Abel made it back to the farm, the twins were doing much better.

"You've done a great job," he told her.

"Does that mean I get a bonus?"

"Whatever you want. Name your price."

Grace thought for a while. A new car would be nice, or a truck. She didn't mention either to Abel. If he thought she wanted one, chances are he would show up with one next weekend, just like he did with Shep. "My normal veterinary fee is enough."

"Then you have to let me take you out to dinner to celebrate. Just business," he insisted.

"Just business." Grace agreed.

Grace settled back into a comfortable routine with Abel, one that didn't demand much from either of them. He came on the weekends allowing her to spend some time with her family, but he also gave her weekly riding lessons and they had a standing date for Saturday nights.

"It's just business," Grace told her parents. "Same as always. He doesn't know anyone here. It gives him a chance to go out, and me too."

Grace was getting progressively better at riding Lady. So much so that Abel now allowed her out of the confines of the corral and into the fields, but not too far yet.

"Once Eleanor is stronger, I'll ride her. We'll be able to go further down the trails," Abel said.

"With the twins and Peanut tagging along?"

"That could be a problem," Abel admitted. "We'll have to stay close to home and ride carefully until they are able to be away from their mothers. It should be easier now that there are three foals to keep each other company."

"You don't let anything get in your way, do you?"

"Not usually. I find there is a solution to every problem, especially if you have enough money to throw at it."

Abel hit Lady on the rump and sent Grace on her way around the pasture at a steady trot. "Before you know it, you'll have gone beyond my ability to teach you," he said when she returned, flushed from the ride.

"What happens then?"

"Maybe we both take lessons."

"That could be arranged." Grace rode Lady back into the corral and waited for Abel till climbing off. For some reason, she was still light-headed at times when she first got off the horse. Not always, but often enough that she didn't want to take a chance. Sometimes it felt like she couldn't catch her breath. She figured it would be gone by now.

"Give it time," Abel told her as he helped her off the mare and steadied her.

Abel attended the horse clinic in April with Grace, participating alongside her. He picked up the techniques Brody McAdams was teaching.

"You're a natural," Brody commented after watching Abel work with Lady. Grace smiled as she watched. She was pleased to see how readily he adapted to different techniques than he had been taught as a teen.

"I guess you can break old bad habits. There is hope for you yet," she told him.

"With the right instructor and the right incentive."

"And that would be?"

"I'm doing it for the business, of course."

Saturday evening there was a barn dance. They skipped their Saturday night dinner at a restaurant for a barbeque at the clinic after returning Lady to the farm. Grace was enjoying meeting local horse owners and when they found out she was a veterinarian her company was even more in demand. She felt at home with them in a way she hadn't felt with any other groups of people, including members of her church.

After the BBQ there was the dance. Abel downed a beer while music filled the air.

"Do you like country music?" Grace asked him.

"Not before this. I think I could learn."

When they played a waltz, he stood up and insisted she join him.

"I'm not much of a dancer." Grace tried to refuse.

"Maybe you haven't found the right partner. Just follow my lead."

Grace struggled at first but as she adjusted to the pressure of his hand on the small of her back, she relaxed and found herself flowing with the music.

"Who told you that you couldn't dance?"

"No one had to."

"When will you stop comparing yourself to your sister?"

Grace ignored his question. "You're quite the dancer."

"Us Barton boys know how to dance. Our mother made sure of that. She used to get us to dance with her in the living room."

"Do you also know how to play piano?"

"No. That was Seth. I never was any good at it. Seth, though, he took to it. It's the only thing I can remember him actually working at."

"So he can be disciplined under the right circumstances."

Abel shrugged then twirled her as the music changed to a line dance. "Do you know this?"

"No, do you?"

"No, but how hard can it be? Let's give it a try."

They bumped into each other and other dancers as they struggled to pick up the steps others did without thinking.

Abel pulled her off the floor to a space where they could try to get the steps down. Both laughed as they messed up. Then Abel started freestyle dancing, swinging her around and under his arms.

"Giving up on the line dance?" Grace asked.

"This is more like it." He swung her one last time as the song ended. Grace hadn't had so much fun dancing since she had danced with Josie as a girl.

The DJ played another slow dance, a classic — "Crazy," sung by Patsy Cline. Grace readily slipped into Abel's arms as they swayed together to the music. This time they didn't talk. Grace was winded from the previous dance. She leaned into Abel's arms for support.

When the song ended, she looked up into his eyes and swallowed. He leaned forward as if to kiss her. She started to tilt her head up to meet his lips, then shook her head, breaking the spell as another line dance began.

"I think I need to sit this one out," Grace said. She was feeling light headed, just like when Abel would help her get down from Lady.

"Do you want anything to drink?"

"No, I'm fine." Grace held onto Abel as he escorted her to a table. "Maybe it's time we call it a night."

"The night is still young," Abel insisted. "The party could go on for hours."

"That's what I'm afraid of. We have to be back tomorrow morning."

"If you insist."

She was staying over at the farm since they needed to get Lady to the clinic first thing in the morning. It made sense. Why drive home to come back the next morning when you have a perfectly good bed here. Grace slipped upstairs and into bed, but she couldn't sleep, not while remembering the dance and the near kiss.

Chapter 39

Each Saturday they took turns choosing restaurants, with Abel preferring the more high-end restaurants and Grace choosing the less formal places. She was finding that she did like going to fancier restaurants now and then.

"A girl could get used to this," she said as she dipped her calamari in sauce and feasted on shrimp and scallops in a seafood alfredo entrée.

"That's what I hope." Abel was unusually quiet this Saturday.

"Is something wrong?" Grace asked as they finished off their meals.

"No. Actually something is right."

"Tell me about it. It's not like you to be so quiet, especially when you have good news."

Abel leaned back and cocked his head. "What would you say to going to Phoenix with me next weekend?"

"Phoenix? Why Phoenix? I'd say, who will take care of the horses? And what about your grandfather?"

"Caroline can handle the horses and Grandpa will be fine on his own for a few days, especially now that we don't have to worry about ice and snow. Shoot, maybe Caroline could stay overnight too, if that's what it takes for you to feel comfortable about being gone."

"But you still haven't told me why."

"My boss is thinking about opening a new factory down there. He wants me to look at some property and check out the potential. He wants me in from the beginning. It'll be bigger than the one I'm currently running and includes a significant pay boost."

"Oh." Grace pushed the remaining noodles from her seafood alfredo around her plate. "Does that mean you would be moving?"

"Only if I accept the position."

"Why, of course you have to accept it. It's the smart thing to do, career-wise."

"Maybe. But my career isn't everything. That's why I want you to come along, check the place out. It won't be all business. There's plenty of open spaces for horseback riding. We can hit the trails when I'm not working." Abel leaned forward and took her hand. "With the money I'll be making we could buy a horse farm. There's plenty of call for veterinarians, especially ones that are good with horses. Hell, you could even buy your own practice if you want."

"Wait. What are you talking about?"

"I don't want to plan for any future that doesn't include you."

Grace withdrew her hand from his, refusing to look up at him.

"Damn it, Grace. Let's stop this pretense. You know this isn't just about business. You know how I feel about you."

He reached over and tipped her chin so she couldn't avoid looking into his eyes. "What I don't know is how you feel about me."

"Maybe I don't know either." She struggled to get the words out as she gazed into his eyes.

"After all this time? How can that be?"

"And now you're talking about Arizona." She turned away, forcing her eyes to leave his. "Couldn't you build a factory in Cascade Falls? We need the industry, especially since those plants pulled out five years ago."

"This isn't about business. It's about you and me." Abel gently turned her head back toward him and looked into her eyes, searching for something. "This isn't about Seth, is it? You're not still holding on to the hope of him showing up?"

"And if I am?" Grace felt a surge of defiance rise inside her, giving her the strength to stand up to him.

"Then maybe I don't know you as well as I thought I did."

"Abel, it's not just Seth. I don't know. I'm not sure how I feel." The defiance slipped away as quickly as it had come, leaving her confused and unsure what to say.

"Well, I know how I feel." Abel stood up and put down money for the bill. "When you figure it out, you let me know." He stormed out, leaving her to sort out what had happened.

Abel was already gone when she came by the farm to pick up Lamar for Sunday dinner. Usually Abel waited for her and they talked before he took off. Not so today. Not that she expected him to wait for her. She knew him well enough to know that once he made up his mind there was no talking to him. One of the traits she disliked in him. She liked to discuss all sides of a disagreement in order to come up with a decision all could live with. Abel, not so much.

"Abel said something about not coming next weekend. Said you knew about it. A business trip," Lamar said on the drive over for Sunday dinner.

"Yes. He has to go to Phoenix to check out some property for his boss."

"That doesn't mean you have to stick around all weekend. I'll be fine by myself. I don't need a babysitter."

Grace decided to take Lamar up on the offer and stay at her parents the weekend Abel went to Phoenix. She didn't want anything to remind her of Abel. As it was, he was all she thought about all week, except when her work distracted her.

She remembered their conversation about Cascade Falls from a while back.

"Have you ever thought about leaving Cascade Falls?" Abel had asked over one of their many dinners.

"Who doesn't? I don't know anyone who grew up here who thought they would live here forever. Especially when I was a teen, living in the shadow of Ashley and Jacob."

"I guess I don't know what that's like. I was the shadow for Seth. What about now?"

"I don't know. After Ashley and Jacob moved away, I didn't see how I could leave my dad. I know he has Ava, but he was lost that first year after Ashley left. Staying here was the least I could do."

"Why?"

"Because I'm the reason my mom died. I have to make it up to him, to everyone." Grace had decided to tell him — something she never shared with anyone outside of the family. She paused before continuing. "My mother had been pregnant with me when the doctor found her cancer. The doctor had wanted her to have an abortion, so they could aggressively treat the cancer, but my mother refused."

"I remember. You told me that."

"My grandmother Mary — she told me it was because my mom loved me so much. She wouldn't let anything happen to me. She risked her life for me. That's how much my mother loved me, Grandma said. Maybe she thought it would make me feel loved, but it didn't. Instead I felt responsible for my mother's death. No one said so, but I'm sure they thought it."

"How do you know that?"

"Why else did Ashley treat me so mean when we were kids, and then, pretty much ran away from home to New York and never came back. It was all because of me."

"Did you talk to Ashley about this? Or anyone?"

"I couldn't. They would have assured me it wasn't my fault. That it was my mother's choice, or that sometimes these things happen. We don't know why, they just do, they would say. Bad things happen to good people."

Grace looked past him as she remembered those days so many years ago, growing up in the shadow of her mom's death.

"It's like Jesus on the cross. Everyone says he died for us. It was supposed to make you realize how much God loves you. But I felt guilty that I was so bad that Jesus had to die for me. I never really understood that — why Jesus had to die because of our sins, or why my mother had to die because of me.

"I had tried talking to my grandmother Esther about it once when I was seven. Why did Jesus have to die for my sins? Am I that bad? I asked her."

"What did she say?"

"She said, 'Oh, sweetheart, of course not.' Then she had closed her eyes, the way she always did when she didn't know what to say. 'You're an old soul,' she said. My grandma had said that before. I never really understood what she meant."

"Maybe that you have a wisdom beyond your years. You think about things that never cross other people's minds."

"Hmmm," Grace pondered. "Maybe. So why did Jesus have to die for my sins?"

"You're asking the wrong person. Jesus and I, we don't talk much."

Grace thought back to that conversation with her grandma. She remembered how her grandmother had smiled and touched Grace's hair. "Grandma said that was for smarter brains than hers to figure out. That Jesus came to show us how to live, to show us the way to Heaven. Everybody dies, but not everybody goes to Heaven.' Then she told me my mom was in Heaven, watching over me."

"I may not know much about religion, but I agree with your grandma."

"Grandma Mary, my mom's mother, she said that my mom gave her life for me, because she loved me so much. Our Pastor always said Jesus gave his life for us and died for our sins because he loved us so much, so I thought my mom had died for my sins."

"Grace, how can you believe that? Your mother didn't die because of you. She had cancer. Sometimes these things happen. It had nothing to do with you." Abel reached for her hand.

"That's what my grandmother said but I didn't believe her. I knew there must be something terribly wrong with me to cause my mother's death. I need to live my life to make up for it. I need to make it up to my family, especially my dad, for what I had done in being born."

"It's thinking like your grandma Mary's that chases people away from church."

"You think so. I don't feel bad about it, just responsible. It's a heavy load."

"One not yours to carry."

Grace shrugged. "Maybe that's why I stayed in Cascade Falls when others left, to make it up to my dad for the loss of my mother."

"That's why you stay? You were just a child. Surely you realize now that it wasn't your fault. Why do you keep punishing yourself? You don't owe it to anybody to stay if you don't want to."

"But what would I do without my grandmother? How could I leave her?" Grace shook her head at the thought. She couldn't leave her grandmother or her family or Cascade Falls. "No, I'll be the eccentric, never-married veterinarian with my cats."

"Correction. You mean your horses."

"That's right. My horses." Grace smiled.

"No, you'll never be that woman. You'll marry."

"How do you know?"

"I just do. I'm good about these things."

Now she wondered if he had paid attention at all when they had talked. He knew how she felt about leaving Cascade Falls. No, he'll take the position and be gone just like Seth. Better for her to get used to it now rather than later. Better to not risk giving her heart to someone else who would leave her.

Chapter 40

Even though Abel wasn't there to give her a riding lesson, she decided to take Lady out for a ride that Saturday. Abel was too bossy anyway. She was capable of riding Lady without his supervision. She went beyond the pasture, seeking out the many trails she knew were in the woods. Her mother used to like to run in the woods around their home. Her dad had told her that once. She understood the attraction but was never able to run. She simply wasn't athletic like her brother and sister. Riding on a horse was about as athletic as she could be. She had been practicing on the yoga ball like Abel had told her to and developing muscle memory. She could tell as she directed Lady into the woods.

Where there had been ice and snow, there were now puddles and mud. She would have to be careful. Maybe she wasn't ready to take the trails yet. But Lady gave her confidence. She seemed as eager to get out of the confines of the corral and pasture as Grace was. Crocuses and daffodils appeared in places along the trail. She wondered how they had gotten there. Maybe Abel's grandmother? Even though she had never met her, she could imagine her escaping the male-dominated household when her grandsons were living with them by going into the woods and planting flowers along the path. Buds were forming on bushes and trees, promise of new life.

She wondered if her mother had ever ridden a horse. She didn't think so. But she would have liked it. Grace was sure of that. Grace felt her presence while she rode in the woods. Her mother would approve. She spent the afternoon exploring the woods before heading back to the corral. This time she wasn't dizzy when she climbed off of Lady. Maybe she was learning.

Her dad and Ava were surprised when she was home Saturday night.

"No date?" her dad asked as they sat down for dinner.

"It's not a date, Dad. It's …"

"I know. It's business. No business date tonight?"

"No. Abel's on a business trip."

"All the more time for us then," Ava smiled as she passed Grace the potatoes.

"Between you, Ashley and Jacob, I don't know if I'll ever get grandchildren," her dad commented. "Not that I'm in a hurry. I just would like to think it will happen sometime. You kids are so focused on your careers. There's more to life than work. Your stepmother and I aren't getting any younger."

"Yes, Dad. I'll see what I can do about that."

"I'm just saying."

As the sole remaining child, Grace felt pressure to fill unmet expectations. Ava tried not to push, but Grace knew Ava would love grandkids.

"There's no such thing as step grandchildren. Only grandchildren," she would say. Ava had been unable to have children after a bout with uterine cancer had led to a hysterectomy before she met Grace's dad. Ava had wanted a family and so had been happy for the ready-made family she had inherited when she married him. Still, Grace knew it hadn't been all Ava had dreamed of. Ashley had never really accepted Ava, not as a stepmother. But then, that was Ashley. Grace didn't know that Ashley accepted anybody, except maybe their dad. For all of her independence, Ashley did care what their dad thought about her.

Grace did love Ava. She was the closest thing to a mother she had, but there was always that spot inside her that longed to know her own mother. It had nothing to do with Ava, everything to do with her.

Chapter 41

Grace picked up each of the litter of six kittens, checking their weight, giving them shots before putting them back into the box they had arrived in. She lingered over the six wriggling bodies, playing with them before turning them back over to their owner. It was one of the perks of being a vet, playing with baby animals. She never missed an opportunity.

"Grace, there's someone here to see you." Adah interrupted her as she made notes on her chart. "Should I send him back?"

"No. I'll be out in a minute." She put the chart away and washed her hands before going out into the waiting area.

"Hello, stranger."

Seth. What was he doing here? "Stranger? I think you deserve that title. You go away, don't write. Don't text. Only call twice."

"I know, and I'm sorry. Let me make it up to you by taking you out for dinner."

Tonight? What did she have to do tonight? Just go home to the farm, check the horses, have dinner with Lamar then watch *The Virginian* before going to bed. Nothing to stop her. "Does your grandfather know you are here?"

"He will. I stopped to see you first. Let me take you away from all of this if just for a night."

How could she say no? She owed him that much, and he owed her as well.

Grace met Seth at the Crab Shack that night.

"I was hoping for music," Seth commented as he sat down.

"Too early in the season." During the summer months the Crab Shack regularly featured a patio party with local bands.

"Too bad. I was hoping to sweep you off your feet on the dance floor." Seth picked up a menu. "What have you done to my grandfather?" he asked as he looked over the selections.

"What do you mean?"

"I mean, instead of being happy to see me, all he worried about was that you would move out. You certainly have charmed him."

"Actually … I was thinking, if you are back, there's no reason for me to stay at the farm. The twins are thriving. They don't need my daily attention. With the warm weather, your grandfather doesn't need me around as much. It was just a matter of time. Your coming home sped it up." The horses didn't need her, but she needed them, she wanted to say. "Besides, you need your room back."

"Keep my room. There's plenty of bedrooms upstairs. If you leave because of me, my grandfather will never forgive me. And then there's Abel. What have you done to him?"

"I don't know what you're talking about?" Grace squirmed at this line of questioning. Seth didn't wait for her to say more. She could always count on Seth to fill a silence. Abel had this annoying habit of waiting for her to respond, not allowing her to escape into silence.

"He sent me the money to fly home. I don't know how you did it, but please let me know. It seems my brother wants me around after all."

"Is that why you are here?"

"It's not the only reason. I wanted to see you. Abel's money made it happen."

Not all that flattering, but Grace let it be. "What have you been doing all this time? Why haven't you answered my texts?"

"I've been out in the South Seas. Have you heard of floating casinos?"

"No. They never came up at vet school."

"I expect not. And you aren't a James Bond fan either, are you? Anyway, they're casinos on cruise ships. Lots of high rollers."

"And you were one of them?"

"I wish. I was just a lowly blackjack dealer. I wasn't able to bankroll a spot at the high stakes table, but I met some of the high rollers. It was just a matter of time before I made a big hit. Then I'd buy my way in."

"Was that what you were doing all this time? Gambling? I thought you were on some great adventure."

"It was a great adventure, money and glitter. At first anyway. All I needed was a stake, but who was going to pay attention to a lowly dealer? So, when Abel contacted me about coming back to Cascade Falls …" Seth shrugged. "Enough of me. What about you? I dare say your life has been more exciting than mine."

"Just working. That's enough excitement for me."

"That's what I love about you, Grace. You are so uncomplicated, easy to get along with."

"You left because of Abel, and now you're back because of Abel. What's up with that?"

"What was I saying about you being easy to get along with," Seth joked. When Grace didn't smile, he added. "What did Abel tell you?"

"Not much. He doesn't like to talk about you."

"No surprise there."

"Why did you leave? Tell me the truth."

"You aren't going to let this go, are you?" Seth rested his cheek on his hand and tried to coax a smile out of her. "Okay. I ran into some money problems. You know how Abel is about money. He wouldn't help me out. I owed some people money. I had to help myself."

That did sound like Abel, Grace thought. "And did you? Did you take care of your problem?"

"I'm working on it."

Grace frowned but didn't respond.

"Don't let this spoil our dinner. I missed you. Maybe the reason I worked so hard, kept so busy, was to get my mind off of you."

"Why do I find that hard to believe?"

"Then believe this. I'm crazy about you, Grace Reese. You're the best thing to come into my life for a long time." Seth reached for her hand.

Grace recoiled at the words. Crazy about her? That's what Abel had said. Brothers. Were they that different? Did they have the same dating repertoire? Use the same words? How could she know who was being truthful?

"I know I've been gone a long time without keeping in touch. If you let me, I'll make it up to you. I'll show you how much I care about you."

She searched his blue eyes for a sign, of what she wasn't sure. How could he look so sincere, sound so sincere, and be lying? Maybe she should give him another chance.

"Grace, I've been a fool. I never should have let Abel chase me off." He continued to hold her hand. "Give me another chance."

Grace turned away. What was she to do? "Okay, I guess." Maybe she owed it to him to give him another chance. "But I think it's best that I move back home."

"Okay, but you have to tell my grandfather." Seth leaned over and gave her a kiss. "Just so you give me a chance. You won't regret it."

But she did.

Chapter 42

Seth wanted to pick up where he left off, but it wasn't the same. Seth's words were hollow, echoing in her ears. What had been fun before, now seemed shallow, empty. All his beautiful words and phrases, his chatter that had been so engaging before, now were empty of meaning.

She surprised her parents when she showed up that night.

"What's up? What are you doing here? Not that we aren't delighted to see you," her dad said.

"Seth is back. No reason for me to stay at the farm. The horses are doing well, there's no reason for me to keep going there every day."

"Seth is back? That's good, isn't it?" Ava asked.

"Yeah, great," Grace mumbled as she climbed the familiar stairs of her childhood home and slept in her bed.

She went to the farm the next night to pick up her things.

"What is going on?" Lamar demanded, stopping her before she went upstairs. "You can't move out like that. What about *The Virginian*?"

"I promise, I'll come over now and then to watch with you. Maybe we can do a *Virginian* marathon some time."

"That's not the same. I didn't ask for that grandson of mine to come back. It's all his fault."

"Why does it have to be someone's fault?"

"Because that's how it is."

Grace shook her head. Apparently, that was the Blackburn way. Someone always had to be at fault.

"I heard that." Seth came up from the barn and joined them. "You see how my grandfather treats me."

"It wasn't my idea, you coming back," Lamar grunted.

"Come on, Gramps. You know you love me." Seth gave him his most endearing smile, one designed to melt the hardest heart. It didn't work on his grandfather any more than it worked on her. At least not now. Not like it had before.

"That doesn't mean I want you to live with me. It's all Abel's fault. Why he had to send for you is beyond me."

"And when is your oldest grandson coming back now that the prodigal grandson is home?"

"I don't know. He didn't say. Since when did either of you boys tell me anything?"

Grace felt a burning in her chest at the mention of Abel. He was gone and it was all because of her, her fault.

"Something about setting up a new factory in Arizona. He didn't know when he would be back," Lamar continued.

Grace didn't know what to say. She had agreed to give Seth a chance, but that was all. Perhaps it was best this way. Time to break with all of the Barton/Blackburn men. If only she didn't miss the horses so much.

Lamar and Seth both insisted she come out and visit the horses.

"There's no reason for you to stop riding Lady," Lamar insisted.

"And I can ride Eleanor once the twins are weaned," Seth added.

She was conflicted where the Blackburn men were concerned, but not about the horses. Somehow, she had to make this work.

Chapter 43

Grace was surprised to see Abel's BMW when she pulled up to the farm the following Saturday. There was another car she recognized, Henry's. Was Caroline here? Grace was going to take Lady out on the trails. That always helped her. But first she had to get her riding boots out of her room. When she heard angry voices coming through the open windows she wanted to disappear into the barn, but not without those boots. The angry voices grew louder as she entered the kitchen. Maybe she could sneak upstairs without being noticed.

Grace tried to slip by the group in the living room when Lamar shouted, "Who's there? Who's in my house?"

Grace stopped and entered the room. "Just me. I'm sorry to interrupt. I wanted to get some more of my stuff from upstairs."

"No, Grace, no need to apologize. I want you to hear for yourself what my brother is doing to me," Seth said.

"More like what you have done to yourself year after year. It's time to face the consequences of your actions." There was Abel, like he always was. Larger than life, in charge. The Abel she remembered from those first days. Not the Abel she had come to know over the past months.

"I'm being disinherited, cut off, and it's all my brother's doing," Seth said.

"What is he talking about?" Grace looked from Abel to Lamar and back again, settling on Abel. "Is this true?"

"It isn't exactly how he's telling it," Abel said.

"Then how is it? Lamar, are you disinheriting your grandson?"

"Let me explain," Lamar started.

"No explanation necessary," Seth said. "It's true, isn't it? Isn't that why you have your lawyer here."

"Yes, but it's not as simple as that," Lamar said.

"You've already spent your inheritance, Seth. You know that," Abel said.

"I'm paying that back," Seth said.

"How? With your gambling money?"

"I just need a break."

"So, you came home to get more money from our grandfather. And I thought it was to see him and Grace. Like you really cared," Abel stated.

"Don't listen to him, Grace." Seth turned to address her. "I do care. About you and my grandfather."

"You only care about the money." Abel was focused on his brother.

"No, that's you. That's all you care about." Seth turned back to confront Abel.

Grace stood frozen while this exchange went on. "Is this true? Is Seth being disinherited?" She asked Henry.

"It is, but what Abel said is also true," Henry explained.

"I don't understand. This is not how families are supposed to be." Grace shook her head. She didn't understand and didn't want to understand. There was that familiar dizziness and shortness of breath, like the air had been knocked out of her. She had to get out of there. "I don't want any part of a family like this." Grace turned to leave.

"Wait, Grace," Abel called to her. "Don't go. This isn't about you. It's family business. This has been going on long before you met any of us."

"And it's going to stay that way, between you." Grace ran out to the barn, threw her gear on Lady and took off across the pasture. She could ride without riding boots. She wanted go as far away from the fighting as possible, as quickly as possible. She hadn't mastered the gallop yet so she set off at a canter.

Something was wrong. Usually riding calmed her down. Not today. Grace felt herself gasp for breath. Lady slowed down then refused to enter the trail.

"What's the matter, girl? Keep going," Grace urged Lady on but she refused to move. Grace felt lightheaded. From behind she heard the sound of hooves galloping across the pasture. She struggled to breathe, then fell forward in the saddle and blacked out.

She was going in and out of consciousness. One minute she thought she felt Abel picking her up and carrying her, then there was some strange man talking to her, but she wasn't sure what he was saying.

"Hang on, Grace. Don't give up. Fight," Grace heard Abel say. What was he talking about?

Then the noise stopped. She was in a field filled with flowers. Lady was grazing nearby. It was quiet and peaceful, filled with colors she had never seen before. There were people at the other side of the pasture waiting for her. She could barely make out the forms but recognized them as humans. Then a beautiful woman in a flowing dress and long light brown hair approached her.

"Mom?" Grace asked. The woman looked like the picture she had seen of her mother, and yet different, transformed.

"Baby Grace." Her mother reached out and stroked her face. "I've been watching you all these years. I'm so proud of the woman you've become."

"Where am I? Am I in Heaven?"

"No, this is a way station. A passage to the world beyond."

"Then I'm dead."

"No, child. Not yet."

"Then where am I? Where is my body?"

"You're at the hospital, in surgery." Her mom pointed and Grace saw someone in an operating room.

"That's me?"

"Yes. It seems when I left you, I left a small hole in your heart. I'm so sorry about that, Grace. It wasn't my choice to leave you, just to give you birth."

"Then why did you leave?"

"Because it was my time."

"Is now my time?"

"That's for you to decide."

"For me to decide?"

"Not everyone is given this choice. You decide whether you want to stay or go back."

Beyond the operating room she saw her dad and Ava sitting together, holding hands and praying. Then she saw a multitude of people praying. Her grandmother and Peter, Aunt Kathleen and Uncle Joe, members of her church, people from town, her clients from the vet clinic, people far away. All were praying.

"Who are all of these people?"

"They are praying for you. Word travels fast in Cascade Falls. All it took was one phone call by your uncle Joe to start the prayer network. Then it spread from there. All of these people care about you. You are more loved than you realize. They are keeping you alive. They are carrying you with their prayers. Can you feel it?"

"Yes, I do. I feel … unburdened, supported, loved."

"That's the power of prayer."

"Then why didn't prayers work for you?"

"They did, my darling child. They gave me you, and gave me two more years with you and your father and Ashley and Jacob. Years I wouldn't have had without prayers."

Grace looked back into the waiting room. Abel sat by himself, unmoving, his head in his hands. Seth paced the room while Lamar sat by her grandmother and Peter.

"I miss you Mom. I missed having a mother all these years."

"That's why God sent Ava into your life, to help fill the gap I left. But no one, not mother, or father, or grandmother or husband or children, can fill all the holes in our heart. Only God can do that. Do you wish to be healed?"

"I don't know. Can I stay here with you?" Grace looked about her. This place of peace and beauty. It was enticing.

"If you wish."

"But what will happen to them if I stay?" She looked back at her family, waiting for her, praying for her.

"It will be hard, but they will manage."

"And if I go back?"

"I will be here waiting for you along with your grandparents. And you will live a life filled with joy and challenges and love. It's your choice. It's not about them, but about you. What do you want?"

What did she want? Did she want life with all of its challenges? How could she leave her dad? Hadn't he suffered enough?

"This isn't about your dad, but about you," her mother's voice sounded in her ears as she looked upon the body on the operating table and the people in the waiting room. "You're not responsible for your father's happiness any more than you're responsible for anyone's happiness. It was not your fault that I died. Do you believe that?"

"How can I when I spent my whole life believing I was?"

Her mother disappeared and a voice spoke, "Do you wish to be healed?"

Did she wish to be healed? She looked at Abel. He would be okay without her, but what did she want? She wanted a life of love and children and grandchildren. She knew her answer.

"Yes," she told the voice.

"Okay, close up," she heard the doctor say. She felt herself being pulled back into her body.

"Wait," she looked for her mother. "Must I lose you again?"

"You never lost me. I'm with you always," she heard her mother's voice as she slipped back into her body and out of consciousness.

Chapter 44

"I think she's coming around," she heard a voice say. Was it her dad? So tired. It was too much effort to open her eyes. She took a deep breath and wiggled a finger. Yes, they still functioned.

"Grace? Can you hear me?" her dad asked.

"Yes." She felt his hand grasp hers. "Where am I?" She kept her eyes closed as she spoke.

"You're in the hospital. You've had heart surgery."

"I know," Grace smiled and opened her eyes. "I saw it. And I saw Mom." Ava turned away when Grace said this.

"You couldn't have. You were sedated the whole time," her dad said.

"And I saw you and Ava." Grace reached for her stepmother's hand and squeezed it. "You were praying for me. And Grandma and Peter and Aunt Kathleen and all the people from church."

"We activated the prayer network," Ava said.

"Where's Grandma?"

"Peter took her home. Once we knew you were going to be okay, we sent everyone home. The doctor said it would probably be hours before you were awake. Everyone went home except for one stubborn man. Do you want to see him?"

Was it Abel or Seth, she wondered. "Like this?"

"You know he won't go away until he sees you."

The doctor came into her room on his rounds. "Good to see you awake. How are you feeling?"

"Like someone broke open my chest and took my heart out."

"It was kind of like that. You have a congenital heart condition. It's been there since your birth, undetected."

"Is that why I've always been so bad at sports?"

"Could be. Did you tire easy?"

"I guess. I didn't know any different."

"I think you'll notice a difference now. We were able to patch you up nicely."

Once the doctor left, her dad went to the waiting room, leaving her with Ava.

"You know, my mom said God sent you to be with me after she died. God sent you not just to my dad but to me too."

"I always believed that. I couldn't believe that I was so lucky to not only find your father but you three kids." Ava wiped the tears from her eyes.

"I believe that too now." Grace reached for Ava's hand. "I'm sorry if I've ever seemed ungrateful or that I didn't love you. You know I love you. You're the only mother I've known. Nothing can change that."

"I know that, Grace. But I appreciate you saying it. I love you more than I ever thought possible. My baby Grace. I don't know what I would do without you. I was so afraid I was losing you."

"How could you lose me? I'm the one who's always around. I'm surprised you aren't tired of me."

"Never." Ava reached over and hugged her, tears running down both of their faces.

"What's going on?" her dad asked when he came back with Abel. "Why all the tears?"

"Just girl talk," Ava said.

"Yeah, mother-daughter stuff you wouldn't understand," Grace added with a smile.

"I won't try." Her dad put his arm around Ava. "We're going for coffee." They stepped out of the room while Abel pulled up a chair next to her bed.

"I'm glad it's you." Grace reached for Abel's hand. "I hear you've been here all night."

"I couldn't leave till I saw you. Seth and my grandfather were here too. They left after the doctor said you were going to be okay. Seth took Grandpa home."

"I'm glad you're here."

"Are you really? I wasn't sure you wanted to see any of us, not after what happened."

"What was that about? Seems like a life-time ago."

"I went after you when you stormed out of the house, rode Eleanor. Grandpa said to let you go, work this out for yourself, but I knew something wasn't right."

"How?"

"I just did. Something in my gut. I couldn't let you ride off. I'm glad I didn't. Who knows when you would have been found if I hadn't come after you? I thought you would be angry with me for following you, but I knew I had to. Fortunately, Lady stopped before you passed out. I was able to get to you before you fell off. She knew too. She knew something was wrong or she would have kept going and you would have fallen off."

"Horses have instincts. They can sense when something's not right."

"I called 911 and carried you back to the house. I was afraid I was going to lose you."

"But you didn't. I'm glad you're here."

"You don't wish it was Seth?"

"No, I wanted it to be you."

"I'm sorry about what you heard the other day, the argument. I didn't want you to hear it that way. And I'm sorry about how I left things between us, rushing off like I did. There's so much I'm sorry about." Abel put both of his hands on hers, cradling her hand with his.

It came back to her, the fighting, riding Lady, blacking out. "Was it true?"

"What did Seth tell you?"

"He said he left because he was in trouble, owed some money, and you wouldn't help him out."

"Did he tell you he paid off his gambling debt by embezzling money from the farm? Grandpa would have lost the farm if I hadn't stepped in."

"Wait. What are you saying?"

"I'm saying, when I came here last Christmas, I had come to save the farm."

"If your grandfather doesn't have any money, how has he been able to pay his bills?"

"I've been paying them. At first I was planning on liquidating the farm and taking my grandfather back to Chicago."

"That would have killed him."

"Exactly. When I realized that, I had to make other plans."

"Does your grandfather know this?"

"Only that Seth had taken some of his money and was going to pay it back."

"Which he hasn't."

"No, but Grandpa doesn't need to know that."

"How long can you keep this up?"

"As long as I have to. I was thinking maybe I could sell the farm and buy Grandpa another one in Phoenix, but there are complications."

"Complications?"

"Yes, a certain young veterinarian who refuses to move." Abel squeezed her hand. "Seth wasn't disinherited. He used up his inheritance and my inheritance. I was taking steps to keep him from taking more."

"But why did you pay for Seth to come back if that was the case? Especially if you thought he might take more money from your grandfather? And why didn't you tell me?"

"Would you have believed me?"

"I don't know."

"I wanted you to make a choice. I didn't want you wondering about Seth."

"But aren't you moving to Phoenix?"

"I realized that you were never going to leave Cascade Falls. That was a problem because there are no jobs for me here."

"You could work for my dad."

Abel smiled his crooked smile and squeezed her hand. "Nah, that wouldn't do. I checked into that closed factory on the outskirts of town. It'll take some doing, but it could work. You're right. There are a lot of people who had been put out of work when it closed. There are good tax incentives for starting a business here, a labor force and property available. All I had to do was put together a business plan and submit it to my boss. It's smaller than the Phoenix factory, but it will do."

"And Phoenix?"

"That's going to happen. It's already in the works. Someone else will take care of the day-to-day operations once it's up and running. I'll fly down periodically to check things out, but I'm not moving there. Phoenix is missing one very important thing." Abel reached over and curled a lock of hair around his finger. "You know, you are beautiful, Dr. Reese."

"No one has said that. Well, except my stepmother."

"You are a classic beauty. I've wanted to see you with your hair down since I first met you." Abel caressed her face and kissed her gently on her lips. "I've wanted to do that as well. The only thing Phoenix is missing is you."

"Is that a proposal?"

"Call it a business proposition."

"Then the answer is yes."

Chapter 45

The next day, Seth walked in carrying a vase filled with a large bouquet of flowers, followed by his grandfather.

"They're beautiful." Grace sat up in the hospital bed. "Thank you."

"The flowers were my idea," Seth placed the vase on the table near her bed.

"Paid for with my money," Lamar added.

Grace smiled. "I thought as much."

"I'm really sorry. We're really sorry, about all that's been going on," Seth stated. "We're sorry we brought you into our family feuds."

"What are you going to do now?" Grace asked.

"I guess I'll be moving on."

"Don't move out on my account," Grace said.

"Naw, it's better this way."

"That means there's an open bedroom if you want it," Lamar added. "*The Virginian* just isn't the same without you."

Once having made up his mind, there was no stopping Abel. He determined that they were to be married, the sooner the better.

"You name it. It'll be the wedding of your dreams. And then we'll honeymoon in Arizona at a ranch where we can ride all day, make love all night." He picked her up and kissed her, his strong arms easily lifting her small frame. "And I'll buy you any house you want. Or better yet, I'll build a house for you."

"If it's all the same to you, I'd be happy living at Blackburn farm in your grandparents' home."

"That's not grand enough."

"I'll let you build me a closed-in riding arena where I can ride all winter and expand the barn for our horses."

"That I can do and more."

And that he did.

Epilogue

Seth moved out. Grace moved back in while Abel built the house of his dreams on the property. Abel wanted to elope. Grace wanted a small wedding with just family and a few friends, but then she remembered all of the people praying for her during her surgery. How could she get married without inviting them?

They married in November at St. Luke's with all of the church attending along with everyone she knew from the vet clinic. They rode through the mountains and desert of Arizona on their honeymoon. Grace marveled at their majesty. The Psalms she had memorized as a child came back to her with a greater power.

"I shall lift mine eyes to the hills, from whence shall come my help."

"Like the mountains surround Jerusalem, so God surrounds his people."

She felt safe, protected and loved.

Back at Blackburn farm, Grace stopped on her way from the barn to look across the land and stare into the starry night.

Abel snuck up behind her and wrapped his arms in front of her, his head easily clearing her head. "You know, you didn't just save my grandfather that night in November, but me too. You are amazing, my Grace."

This time when Grace looked across the field at the early snow and smelled the cool crisp air, she didn't smell death, but life.

Note to the Reader

Make an author extremely happy!

Did you enjoy reading this book? If so, please leave a review. Your comments would be appreciated and mean so much to me in terms of helping others notice my book. You, the reader, have the power to make or break a book in this day of emarketing and social media.

Thank you so much for reading *Amazing*. Continue to follow the adventures of the Reese family children in the next book in the series, *Prima Ballerina*!

Patricia M. Robertson

Other Novels by Patricia M. Robertson

Dreamweavers – Dream again, wherever you are in your life.

Buying Time – Visit the peace movement during the Cold War era of Ronald Regan, SDI (Strategic Defense Initiative) and MAD (Mutually Assured Destruction).

Land of Deep Waters - Honduras, land of deep waters, a country torn apart by civil unrest, violence and poverty: Is it possible to go back?

Magnificent Failure - Is it possible to start over? Failures in the eyes of the world and their own eyes, Diane and Jake found each other.

Dancing Through Life Series

Dancing on a High Wire – What do you do when life knocks you off balance? Join Sara, Joy and Esther as each seeks to find a "new normal" and regain their balance on this high wire we call life.

Still Dancing - Some phone calls we love, others we hate, like the ones Pastor Joe receives from his daughter's school. Or the one Dale received at work, letting him know his wife, Joy, had fallen and was in route to the hospital by ambulance. Could her cancer be back?

A Slow Waltz - The road to healing from loss is a slow one, sometimes going backward and sideways before going forward. Sometimes the biggest barrier to healing lies within us. Join Dale, Kathleen, Ava and others as they journey to forgiveness and healing.

An Irish Slip Step - Kathleen knew about slipping up. As did Chloe's, whose life was knocked off balance by an unplanned pregnancy. And then there was that fiery red-head, Mary Helen, who fell in love with an American soldier. Was it a slip-step or one of life's fortuitous missteps that brought them precisely where they were meant to be?

Delicious Secrets - A church secretary was the last job Marcy would have chosen, but she makes the best of it by entertaining herself with real and imagined secrets about church members, until she stumbles upon a secret she would rather not know. Once known, there was no turning back.

Beautiful Questions - Some questions are so big, they can take a lifetime to answer. They are big enough for you to live in, walk around in them, taste them, touch them, and test them. They are beautiful questions. What are the beautiful questions in your life? Join Gwen and others as they ask beautiful questions.

Lyrical Dance - What do you do when all you've ever known about yourself, what gave your life meaning, is wiped away? How do you get it back?

Freedom Dance - All of her life, Letty has struggled to fit in. There is the middle-class world of her parents, the white middle-class world of her friends, and the poverty-stricken world of her cousins. Will she ever find her place in the world?

Man of the Month – The last place Gwen wanted to do her internship was her home town, Cascade Falls. But her father's heart attack and recuperation required her presence. Even worse, her mother starts the "Man of the Month Club" to find eligible young men for Gwen to date until she finds Mr. Right and settles down in Cascade Falls. Would she ever escape her home town?

Rebound - Jacob was the rebound king, both on the court and off. He got up after being knocked down as if nothing had happened. He picked up and dropped women as quickly as the ball in a basketball game. Until he met the one woman who was impervious to his charms. Had he finally found a love to last a lifetime, only to lose her?

About the Author

Patricia M. Robertson is an author, speaker and spiritual director, who is committed to helping individuals find God in their every day experience. She also is author of a companion non-fiction book to *Still Dancing, Walking with Families through the Dying Process*, as well as *Walking with Families through Grief,* a companion to *A Slow Waltz*.

She has written other non-fiction books and writes a weekly blog and monthly newsletter. She has a Doctor of Ministry and over thirty-five years of experience in ministry to families. She currently is enjoying her own love story with her husband, Jack, grown children and grandchildren. For more information about her ministry, go to www.patriciamrobertson.com.

Prima Ballerina

Patricia M. Robertson

Ashley handed her driver's license and credit card to the counter person at Avis rental cars. It had already been a long day and it wasn't over. Tired from the afternoon performance and flight from New York, all Ashley wanted was to be back home in her apartment, icing her feet with a bag of frozen peas, sipping wine and preparing to sleep in her cozy bed covered by her down comforter. Instead, here she was, waiting for a rental car in Detroit. The sun was setting by the time her flight arrived at Metro Airport. She had another hour of driving ahead of her. Why had she opted for this flight instead of waiting till tomorrow?

"New York," the woman muttered.

"Yes, is that a problem?" Ashley balanced the two sets of luggage she had managed to drag from the luggage carousel, then on to the shuttle bus for a ride to the rental place. What a pain. Was there something wrong with having a New York driver's license? She had traveled abroad and had less trouble going through customs than she was having getting a rental car. Of course, those times she had been travelling with her dance company. The company took care of all the arrangements. All she had to do was pack her bag, make sure she had her passport, and show up on time to be picked up and transported to the airport.

No need for a rental car. No need for a car period living in New York City. She used cabs and the subway for all of her transportation needs. And for those excursions out of the city, to upstate New York and the Catskills, or for a weekend in Vermont, cars were taken care of by her current beau. No need to worry herself with driving.

It had been years since she was behind the wheel of a car.

The woman ignored her question. "Do you have proof of insurance? If you don't have insurance you will have to purchase ours."

"Of course, I don't have insurance. I don't own a car. Why would I have insurance?"

"You'll need to sign up for insurance. Here are the options ..." The woman peered at her over her glasses, tapping her fingers while Ashley read over the paperwork.

"If you need more time, step aside so I can help the next customer."

Why hadn't Michael told her about this? "No, just give me what I need to get on the road."

"We can't let just anybody drive away in one of our cars."

"Apparently you don't know who I am." Oh, that's right. She was no longer in New York.

"Then why do you need a rental? Last I checked, there was no limo waiting to pick you up."

She had her there. Ashley looked at the woman's nametag. Shirley. Ashley signed up for what appeared to be the basic insurance and handed Shirley her credit card. "Look, Shirley, just do whatever you have to do to get me on the road."

Shirley looked over the papers, charged her credit card and handed her a set of keys with a map showing where her rental car was located.

Ashley looked at the key fob that had been placed in her hand. How hard could it be? "Where's the key?" Ashley stared at the fob. There was no key that she could tell.

"It's keyless entry. You have driven cars with push button ignitions, haven't you?" Shirley looked over her glasses at Ashley again, a sneer formed on her lips and reverberated in the question.

How dare she? Did she know who she was talking to? She was Ashley Reese, prima ballerina with one of New York's premiere ballet companies, affectionately referred to as "The Company" by its dancers.

"When you're close enough to the car, the door unlocks automatically. You push in the ignition to start. All you have to do is have the fob in the car to drive."

"Sure. Of course." Ashley had no idea. But there was no way she was going to let this woman know that. Had cars changed that much since she had last driven one?

"Next," Shirley dismissed her.

Now all she had to do was find the car. How hard could that be? She looked at the map. It showed her where her car was, but not how to get to the parking lot. No way she was going to ask Shirley how to get there. She looked for someone to ask, saw the couple that had been behind her at the counter and followed them. No problem.

Her dad had offered to pick her up at the airport. He would have done it in a heartbeat, but she would have none of that.

"And appear like a helpless school girl who can't even drive a car? And then be dependent on others and their cars the whole time I'm there?"

"Ava and I'd be happy to drive you. Gives us more time with you. Or you could drive one of our cars."

"Dad, I've been living on my own in New York for fifteen years. I think I can manage to find my way home from the airport."

"It's not that I think you can't. It's just . . . you're so grown-up. I have so few opportunities to treat you like a daughter. Humor me. Let me do this." Ashley heard the kindness in his voice. It was almost enough to get her to give in. What would it hurt?

But Ashley prevailed as she did most times, fighting the urge to give in to her dad. How hard could it be? It's like riding a bike, right? Once you know how, you never forget.

Maybe that had been a mistake.

Learning to drive hadn't been a high priority back in high school. She had taken a drivers' training course and spent the required amount of time using her learner's permit, driving with another licensed driver in the car, until she got her license. Once acquired, it no longer seemed that important. After that, her focus had been on getting out of Cascade Falls as quickly as possible. She drove when she was home on breaks, but since she started dancing with The Company ten years ago, she hadn't been home. That was a long time to go without driving. She kept her license up-to-date as an ID.

Ashley found the car, threw her suitcases in the back seat, then sat down behind the wheel and stared at the dashboard. Her right foot searched for pedals. Yes, the gas and the brake were in the same place she remembered. There was a button where she had expected to find the ignition. She pushed the button in and was surprised as the car came to life. Nothing to it.

As she turned on the navigation on her phone, her parent's address popped up. All she had to do was get on I-94 going west and she'd be home before she knew it. She adjusted the mirrors, put the car in reverse, backed out and was on her way.

Bright lights of moving cars startled her as she pulled out of the parking area. Where had all these vehicles come from? She eased the car into the right lane only to be told to cross three lanes of traffic and stay to the left by the automated voice. How was she going to cross three lanes of traffic?

Horns blared as she slowed down to move into the next lane, stopping traffic behind her and cutting off traffic in the lanes. She made it into the far lane and thought she was home free — but then she missed an exit and ended up circling the airport.

Good practice, she told herself as she circled through the airport twice before finding I-94. She let out a sigh of relief when she saw the entrance ramp for I-94 West to Chicago. Finally. She veered right onto the ramp and onto I-94 where a surge of truck traffic blocked her from merging onto the highway. She remained in the merging lane while the trucks zoomed by, rattling her Ford Fiesta. "Merge left onto I-94

West," the voice of her navigation system kept repeating. She still had room in her lane, Ashley thought as she crawled along looking for her opening, until she saw that the entrance lane had turned into an exit lane. She had no option but to exit.

"Recalculating, recalculating," the voice repeated. Ashley knew that message from her three trips around the airport. She took a right after the exit, staring into the darkness for road signs to let her know where she was.

"Make a U-turn at the first opportunity," the voice stated.

Make a U-turn? Where was she going to do that?

Ashley turned down a road lined with hotels, pulled into the drive of the closest one and took a deep breath as she assessed the situation. Maybe she should get a room and continue home tomorrow in daylight? But no. She was Ashley Reese, prima ballerina. She had this.

She went back the way she had come in, turned left on the road and saw the entrance ramp. This time traffic had cleared enough so she was able to get into the lane. Easy! She was on her way.

The prodigal daughter would soon be home.